A NOTE ON THE AUTHOR

PATRICK MODIANO was born in Paris in 1945 in the immediate aftermath of World War Two and the Nazi occupation of France, a dark period which continues to haunt him. After passing his baccalauréat, he left full-time education and dedicated himself to writing, encouraged by the French writer Raymond Queneau. From his very first book to his most recent, Modiano has pursued a quest for identity and some form of reconciliation with the past. His books have been published in forty languages and among the many prizes they have won are the Grand Prix du Roman de l'Académie française (1972), the Prix Goncourt (1978) and the Austrian State Prize for European Literature (2012). In 2014 he was awarded the Nobel Prize for Literature.

LA PLACE DE
L'ÉTOILE

Patrick Modiano

Translated from the French by Frank Wynne

BLOOMSBURY
LONDON · OXFORD · NEW YORK · NEW DELHI · SYDNEY

Bloomsbury Paperbacks
An imprint of Bloomsbury Publishing Plc

50 Bedford Square   1385 Broadway
London   New York
WC1B 3DP   NY 10018
UK   USA

www.bloomsbury.com

BLOOMSBURY and the Diana logo are trademarks of Bloomsbury Publishing Plc

La Place de l'Étoile was originally published in France in 1968
by Éditions Gallimard, Paris, as *La Place de l'Étoile*
La Place de l'Étoile © Éditions Gallimard, Paris, 1968. New edition modified by the author in 1985
English translation © Frank Wynne, 2015

Patrick Modiano has asserted his right under the Copyright, Designs and Patents Act, 1988, to be
identified as the Author of this work.

This book is supported by the
Institut français (Royaume-Uni) as
part of the Burgess programme
(www.frenchbooknews.com)

Extract from *In Search of Lost Time Volume IV: Sodom and Gomorrah*, by Marcel Proust,
translated by C. K. Moncrieff & Terence Kilmartin and revised by D. J. Enright.
Copyright © 1981 by Chatto & Windus and Penguin Random House LLC. Revisions to the
translation copyright © 1992 by D. J. Enright. Used by permission of Modern Library, an
imprint of The Random House Publishing Group, a division of Penguin Random House LLC.

British Library Cataloguing-in-Publication Data
A catalogue record for this book is available from the British Library.

ISBN: PB: 978-1-4088-6795-2
ePub: 978-1-4088-6796-9

2 4 6 8 10 9 7 5 3 1

Typeset by Integra Software Services Pvt. Ltd.
Printed and bound in Great Britain by CPI Group (UK) Ltd, Croydon CR0 4YY

To find out more about our authors and books visit www.bloomsbury.com. Here you will find extracts,
author interviews, details of forthcoming events and the option to sign up for our newsletters.

For Rudy Modiano

In June 1942, a German officer approaches a
young man and says, 'Excuse me, monsieur,
where is the Place de l'Étoile?'
The young man gestures to the left side of
his chest.
(Jewish story)

I

This was back when I was frittering away my Venezuelan inheritance. Some talked of nothing but my beautiful youth and my black curls, others called me every name under the sun. Rereading an article about me written by Léon Rabatête in a special edition of *Ici la France*: ' . . . how long do we have to suffer the antics of Raphäel Schlemilovitch? How long can this Jew brazenly flaunt his neuroses and his paroxysms with impunity from le Touquet to Cap d'Antibes, from le Baule to Aix-les-Bains? Once again, I ask: how long can dagos of his ilk be allowed to insult the sons of France? How long must we go on washing our hands of this Jewish scum . . . ?' Writing about me in the same newspaper, Doctor Bardamu spluttered: ' . . . Schlemilovitch? . . . Ah, the foul-smelling mould of the ghettos! . . . that shithouse lothario! . . . runt of a foreskin! . . . Lebano-ganaque scumbag! . . . rat-a-tat . . . wham! . . . Consider this the Yiddish gigolo . . . this rampant arsefucker of Aryan girls! . . . this brazenly Negroid abortion! . . . frenzied Abyssinian young nabob! . . . Help! . . . La-di-da-di-da! . . . rip his guts out . . . hack his balls off! . . . Preserve the Doctor from this spectacle! . . . in the name of God, crucify him! . . . this foreign trash with his filthy cocktails . . . this Jewboy with his international palaces! . . . his orgies *made in Haifa*! . . .

Cannes!... Davos!... Capri *e tutti quanti*!... vast devoutly Hebrew brothels!... Preserve us from this circumcised fop!... from his salmon-pink Maserati!... his Sea of Galilee yachts!... his Sinai neckties!... may his Aryan slave girls rip off his prick!... with their perfect French teeth... their delicate little hands... gouge out his eyes!... death to the Caliph!... Revolution in the Christian harem!... Quick!... Quick!... refuse to lick his balls!... to pander to him for his dollars!... Free yourselves!... stay strong, Madelon!... otherwise you'll have the Doctor sobbing!... wasting away!... oh hideous injustice!... It's a plot by the Sanhedrin!... They want the Doctor dead!... take my word for it!... the Israelite Central Consistory!... the Rothschild Bank!... Cahen d'Anvers!... Schlemilovitch!... help Doctor Bardamu, my little girls!... save me!...'

The Doctor never did forgive me for the copy of *Bardamu Unmasked* I sent him from Capri. In the essay, I revealed the sense of wonder I felt when, as a Jewish boy of fourteen, I read *The Journey of Bardamu* and *The Childhood of Louis-Ferdinand* in a single sitting. Nor did I shrug off the author's anti-Semitic pamphlets as good Christian souls do. Concerning them, I wrote: 'Doctor Bardamu devotes considerable space in his work to the Jewish Question. This is hardly surprising: Doctor Bardamu is one of us; he is the greatest Jewish writer of all time. This is why he speaks of his fellow Jews with passion. In his purely fictional works, Dr Bardamu reminds us of our Race brother Charlie Chaplin in his taste for poignant details, his touching, persecuted characters . . . Dr Bardamu's sentences are even more "Jewish" than the rococo prose of Marcel Proust: a plaintive, tearful melody, a little showy, a tad histrionic . . .' I concluded: 'Only the Jews can truly understand one of their own, only a Jew can speak perceptively about Dr Bardamu.' By way of response, the doctor sent me an insulting letter: according to him, with my orgies and my millions I was orchestrating the global Jewish conspiracy. I also sent him my *Psychoanalysis of Dreyfus* in which I categorically affirmed his guilt; a novel idea coming from a Jew. I elaborated the following theory: Alfred Dreyfus passionately loved the France of Saint Louis, of Joan of Arc, of Les Chouans. But France, for her part, wanted nothing to do with the Jew Dreyfus. And so he betrayed her, as a man might avenge himself on a scornful woman with spurs fashioned like fleurs-de-lis. Barrès, Zola and Deroulède knew nothing of such doomed love.

Such an analysis no doubt disconcerted the doctor. I never heard from him again.

The paroxysms of Rabatête and Bardamu were drowned out by the praise heaped upon me by society columnists. Most of them cited Valery Larbaud and Scott Fitzgerald: I was compared to Barnabooth, I was dubbed 'The Young

Gatsby'. In magazine photographs, I was invariably shown with my head tilted slightly, gazing towards the horizon. In the columns of the romance magazines, my melancholy was legendary. To the journalist who buttonholed me on the steps of the Carlton, the Normandy or the Miramar, I ceaselessly proclaimed my Jewishness. In fact, my actions ran counter to the virtues cultivated by the French: discretion, thrift, work. From my oriental forebears, I inherited my dark eyes, a taste of exhibitionism and luxury, an incurable indolence. I am not a son of France. I never knew a life of grandmothers who made jam, of family portraits and catechism. And yet, I constantly dream of provincial childhoods. My childhood is peopled by English governesses and unfolds on beaches of dubious repute: in Deauville, Miss Evelyn holds my hand. Maman neglects me in favour of polo players. She kisses me goodnight when I am in bed, but sometimes she does not take the trouble. And so, I wait for her, I no longer listen to Miss Evelyn and the adventures of David Copperfield. Every morning, Miss Evelyn takes me to the Pony Club. Here I take my riding lessons. To make maman happy, I will be the most famous polo player in the world. The little French boys know all the football teams. I think only of polo. I whisper to myself the magic words, 'Laversine', 'Cibao-La Pampa', 'Silver Leys', 'Porfirio Rubirosa'. At the Pony Club, I am often photographed with the young princess Laïla, my fiancée. In the afternoons, Miss Evelyn takes us to La Marquise de Sevigné for chocolate umbrellas. Laïla prefers lollipops. The ones at La Marquise de Sevigné are oblong and have a pretty stick.

Sometimes I manage to give Miss Evelyn the slip when she takes me to the beach, but she knows where to find me: with ex-king Firouz or Baron Truffaldine, two grown-ups who are friends of mine. Ex-king Firouz buys me pistachio sorbets and gushes: 'You have a sweet tooth like myself, my little Raphäel!' Baron Truffaldine is always alone and sad at the Bar au Soleil. I walk up to his table and stand in front of him. The old man launches into interminable anecdotes featuring characters called Cléo de Merode, Otéro, Émilienne d'Alençon, Liane de Pougy, Odette de Crécy. Fairies probably, like the ones in the tales of Hans Christian Andersen.

The other props that clutter my childhood include orange beach parasols, the Pré-Catalan, Hattemer Correspondence Courses, *David Copperfield*, the Comtesse de Ségur, my mother's apartment on the quai Conti and three photos taken by Lipnitzki in which I am posed next to a Christmas tree.

Then come the Swiss boarding schools in Lausanne and my first crushes. The Duisenberg given me for my eighteenth birthday by my Venezuelan uncle Vidal glides through the blue evening. I pass through a gate and drive through the park that slopes gently to Lake Leman and leave the car by the steps leading up to a villa twinkling with lights. Girls in pale dresses are waiting for me on the lawn. Scott Fitzgerald has written more elegantly that I ever could about these 'parties' where the twilight is too tender, the laughter and the shimmering lights too harsh to bode well. I therefore recommend you read the author, you will have a precise idea of the parties of my adolescence. Failing that, read *Fermina Marquez* by Larbaud.

If I shared the pleasures of my cosmopolitan classmates in Lausanne, I did not quite resemble them. I often went off to Geneva. In the silence of the Hôtel des Bergues, I would read the Greek bucolic poets and strive to elegantly translate the *Aeneid*. In the course of one such retreat, I made the acquaintance of a young aristocrat from Touraine, Jean-François Des Essarts. We were the same age and I was astounded by the breadth of his knowledge. At our first meeting, he recommended that I read – in no particular order – Maurice Scève's *Délie*, Corneille's comedies, the memoirs of Cardinal de Retz. He initiated me into the grace and the subtleties of French.

In him, I discovered precious qualities: tact, generosity, a great sensitivity, a scathing wit. I remember Des Essarts used to compare our friendship to the one between Robert de Saint-Loup and the narrator of *In Search of Lost Time*. 'You're a Jew, like the narrator,' he would say, 'and I'm related to the Noailles, the Rochechouart-Mortemarts and the La Rochfoucaulds like Robert de Saint-Loup. Don't worry, for a century now the French aristocracy have had a soft spot for Jews. I'll show you a few pages by Drumont in which this upstanding man castigates us for it bitterly.'

I decided never to return to Lausanne and, without the slightest compunction, sacrificed my cosmopolitan friends for Des Essarts.

I turned out my pockets. I had exactly a hundred dollars. Des Essarts did not have a *centime* to his name. Even so, I suggested he give up his job as sports correspondent for *La Gazette de Lausanne*. I had just remembered that, during a weekend spent in England, some friends had dragged me to a manor near Bournemouth to see a collection of old automobiles. I tracked down the name of the collector, Lord Allahabad, and sold him my Duisenberg for fourteen thousand pounds. On such a sum we could live decently for a year without having to depend on having money wired by my uncle Vidal.

We moved into the Hôtel des Bergues. I still have dazzling memories of this early period of our friendship. In the morning, we would loiter among the antique dealers of old Geneva. Des Essarts passed on to me his passion for bronzes. We bought some twenty pieces which cluttered up our rooms, among them a verdigris allegory representing 'Toil' and a pair of magnificent stags. One afternoon, Des Essarts informed me that he had acquired a bronze footballer:

'Parisian snobs will soon be falling over themselves to pay big money for these things. Take my word for it, my dear Raphäel! If it were up to me, the thirties style would be back in vogue.'

I asked him why he had left France:

'Military service did not suit my delicate constitution,' he explained, 'so I deserted.'

'We shall fix that,' I told him. 'I promise to find you a skilled craftsman here in Geneva to make you false papers: you'll be able to go back to France anytime you like without having to worry.'

The dubious printer we managed to track down produced a Swiss birth certificate and passport in the name Jean-François Lévy, born in Geneva on July 30, 194—.

'Now I'm one of your lot,' said Des Essarts, 'I was bored of being a goy.'

I immediately decided to send an anonymous confession to the left-wing Paris newspapers. I wrote as follows:

'Since November last, I have been guilty of desertion but the French military authorities have decided it is safer to hush up my case. I told them what today I am declaring publicly. I am a JEW and the army that spurned the services of Capitaine Dreyfus can do without mine. I have been condemned for failing to fulfil my military duties. Time was, the same tribunal condemned Alfred Dreyfus because he, a JEW, had dared to choose a career in the army. Until such time as this contradiction can be explained to me, I refuse to serve as a second-class soldier in an army that, to this day, has wanted nothing to do with a Maréchal Dreyfus. I urge all young French Jews to follow my example.'

I signed it: JACOB X.

As I had hoped, the French left feverishly took up the moral dilemma of Jacob X. It was the third Jewish scandal in France after the Dreyfus affair and the Finaly Affair. Des Essarts got in on the game, and together we wrote a dazzling 'Confession of Jacob X' which was serialised in a Parisian weekly: Jacob X had been taken in by a French family whose name he chose not to reveal consisting of a Pétainist colonel, his wife, a former canteen worker, and three sons, the eldest of whom joined the mountain infantry, the second the marines, the youngest had been accepted to the military academy of Saint-Cyr.

The family lived in Paray-le-Monial and Jacob X had grown up in the shadow of the basilica. The living room walls were bedecked with portraits of Gallieni, of Foch and Joffre, with Colonel X's military cross and a number of *francisques*. Under the influence of his adoptive family, the young Jacob X came to worship the French army: he, too, would go to Saint-Cyr, he, like Pétain, would be a maréchal. At school, Monsieur C., the history master, discussed the Dreyfus Affair. Before the war, Monsieur C. had held an important post in the PPF. He was well aware that Colonel X had betrayed Jacob X's parents to the Germans and his life had been spared after the liberation only because he had adopted the little Jew. Monsieur C. despised the *pétainisme* of the X family: he revelled in the idea of causing dissension within the family. After the lesson, he called Jacob X over and whispered: 'I'm sure you find the Dreyfus Affair very upsetting. A young Jewish boy like you must feel personally affronted by such injustice.' To his horror, Jacob X discovers he is a Jew. Having identified with Maréchal Foch, with Maréchal Pétain, he suddenly discovers that he is like Capitaine Dreyfus. And yet he does not seek to avenge himself through treason like Dreyfus. He receives his call-up papers and can see no way out but to desert.

The confession divided French Jews. The Zionists advised Jacob X to emigrate to Israel. There he could legitimately aspire to the baton of a maréchal. The assimilated, self-loathing Jews claimed that Jacob X was an agent provocateur in the pay of neo-Nazis. The Left passionately defended the young deserter. Sartre's article, 'Saint Jacob X: Actor and Martyr' sparked the offensive. Everyone will remember the most germane passage: 'Tomorrow, he will think of himself as a Jew, but a Jew in abjection. Beneath the glowering stares of Gallieni, Joffre and Foch whose portraits hang on the walls of the living room, he will become a vulgar deserter, this boy who, since childhood, had worshipped the French army, "La Casquette du père Bugeaud" and Pétain's *francisques*. In short, he will experience the delicious shame of feeling Other, that is to say Evil.'

Various pamphlets circulated demanding that Jacob X return in triumph. A public meeting was held at la Mutualité. Sartre pleaded with Jacob X to forego anonymity, but the obstinate silence of the deserter discouraged even the best intentioned.

We take our meals at le Bergues. In the afternoons, Des Essarts works on a book about pre-revolutionary Russian cinema. As for me, I translate Alexandrian poets. We settle on the hotel bar to work on these trivial tasks. A bald man with eyes like embers regularly comes and sits at the table next to ours. One afternoon, he speaks to us, staring at us intently. Suddenly, from his pockets, he takes an old passport and proffers it. To my astonishment I read the name Maurice Sachs. Alcohol makes him talkative. He tells us of his misadventures since 1945, the date of his supposed death. He was, successively, a Gestapo officer, a GI, a cattle trader in Bavaria, a broker in Anvers, a brothel-keeper in Barcelona, a clown in a Milan circus under the stage name Lola Montès. He finally settled in Geneva where he runs a small bookshop. To celebrate this chance meeting, we drink until three in the morning. From that day forth, we and Maurice are inseparable and we solemnly vow to keep secret the fact that he is alive.

We spend our days sitting behind piles of books in the back office of his bookshop, listening as he brings 1925 to life for us. In a voice made gravelly by alcohol, Maurice talks about Gide, Cocteau, Coco Chanel. The adolescent of the Roaring Twenties is now a fat old man gesticulating wildly at the memory of Hispano-Suiza automobiles and Le Boeuf sur le Toit.

'Since 1945, I've been living on borrowed time,' he confides, 'I should have died when the moment was right, like Drieu la Rochelle. Trouble is: I'm a Jew, I have the survival instincts of a rat.'

I make a note of this comment and, the following day, bring Maurice a copy of my study *Drieu and Sachs: where primrose paths lead*. In the study, I show how two young men in 1925 lost their way because they lack depth of character: Drieu, the grand young man of Sciences-Po, a French petit bourgeois fascinated by convertibles, English neckties and American girls, who passed himself off as a hero of the Great War; Sachs, a young Jew of great charm and dubious morals, the product of a putrid post-war generation. By 1940, tragedy is sweeping Europe. How will our two bright young things react? Drieu remembers that he was born on the Cotentin Peninsula and spends four years singing the 'Horst-Wessel-Lied' in a shrill falsetto. For Sachs, occupied Paris is an Eden where he can lose himself in wild abandon. This is a Paris that offers him pleasures much more intense that the Paris of

1925. Here it is possible to traffic in gold, rent apartments and sell off the furniture, trade ten kilos of butter for a sapphire, convert the sapphire into scrap metal, etc. Night and fog mean there is no need for explanations. But above all, there is the thrill of being able to buy his life on the black market, to purloin each beat of his heart, to feel himself the prey in a hunt! It is difficult to imagine Sachs in the Résistance, fighting alongside French petty bureaucrats for the reinstatement of morality, legality and the light of day. Towards 1943, when he can feel the baying pack and the ratcatchers moving in, he signs up as a volunteer in Germany and, later, becomes an active member of the Gestapo. I have no wish to upset Maurice: I have him die in 1945 and pass over in silence his various incarnations from 1945 to the present day. I conclude thus: 'Who would have thought that, twenty years later, the charming young man of 1925 would be savaged by dogs on the plains of Pomerania?'

Having read my study, Maurice says:
'It's very neat, Schlemilovitch, the parallel between Drieu and myself, but I have to say I would prefer a parallel between Drieu and Brasillach. Compared to them I was a mere prankster. Write something for tomorrow morning and I shall tell you what I think.'

Maurice is delighted to be mentoring a young man. Doubtless he is remembering the first visits he made, his heart pounding, to Gide and Cocteau. He is greatly pleased with my *Drieu and Brasillach*. I attempted to address the following question: what were the motives that prompted Drieu and Brasillach to collaborate?

The first part of this study was entitled: 'Pierre Drieu la Rochelle, or the eternal love affair between the SS and the Jewess.' One subject recurs frequently in the novels of Drieu: the Jewish woman. That noble Viking, Gilles Drieu, had no hesitation about pimping Jewish women, a certain Myriam for example. His attraction to Jewish women can also be explained in the following manner: ever since Walter Scott, it has been understood that Jewish women are meek courtesans who submit to the every whim of their Aryan lords and masters. In the company of Jewish women Drieu had the illusion of being a crusader, a Teutonic knight. Up to this point, there was nothing very original in my analysis, Drieu's commentators have all focussed on the role of the Jewess in his writings. But Drieu as collaborator? This I explain easily: Drieu was fascinated by Doric masculinity. In June 1940, the real Aryans, the true warriors, descend on Paris: Drieu quickly shucks off the Viking costume he hired to violate the young Jewish girls of Passy. He discovers his true nature: beneath the steely blue gaze of the SS officers, he softens, he melts, he suddenly feels an oriental languidness. All too soon, he is swooning into the arms of the conquerors. After their defeat, he immolates himself. Such passivity, such a taste for Nirvana are surprising in a man from Normandy.

The second part of my study was entitled 'Robert Brasillach, or the Maid of Nuremberg.' 'There were many of us who slept with Germany,' he confessed, 'and the memory of it will remain sweet.' His impulsiveness reminds me of the young Viennese girls during the *Anschluss*. As German soldiers marched along Ringstraße, girls dressed up in their chicest dirndls to shower them with roses. Afterwards they strolled in the Prater with these blonde angels. Then came a magical twilight in the Stadtpark where they kissed an SS Totenkopf while murmuring Schubert lieder in his ear. My God, how handsome the youths were on the far side of the Rhine! How could anyone not fall in love with Hitler Youth Quex? In Nuremberg, Brasillach could scarcely believe his eyes: the bronzed muscles, the pale eyes, the tremulous lips of the *Hitlerjugend* and the cocks you could sense straining in the torrid night, as pure a night as falls over Toledo from Los Cigarrales . . . I met Robert Brasillach at the École Normale Supérieure. He affectionately referred to me as his 'dear little Moses', or his 'dear little Jew'. Together, we discovered the Paris of Pierre Corneille and René Clair, dotted with pleasant bistros where we would sip glasses of white wine. Robert would talk maliciously about our teacher André Bellessort and we would plan delightful little pranks. In the afternoons, we would 'coach' dim-witted, pretentious young Jewish numbskulls. At night, we would go to the cinematograph or share with our fellow classmates a copious *brandade de morue*. Towards midnight, we would drink the iced orangeades Robert so loved because they reminded him of Spain. This, then, was our youth, the deep morning never to be regained. Robert embarked on a brilliant career as a journalist – I remember an article he wrote about Julien Benda. We were strolling through the Parc Montsouris and, in his manly voice, our own 'Grand Meaulnes' was denouncing Benda's intellectualism, his Jewish obscenity, his Talmudist's senility. 'Excuse me,' he said to me suddenly, 'I've probably offended you. I'd forgotten you were an Israelite.' I blushed to the tips of my fingers. 'No, Robert, I'm an honorary goy! Surely you must know that Jean Lévy, Pierre-Marius Zadoc, Raoul-Charles Leman, Marc Boasson, René Riquieur, Louis Latzarus, René Gross – all Jews like me – were passionate supporters of Maurras? Well, I want to work at *Je suis partout*, Robert! Please, introduce me to your friends! I'll write the anti-Semitic column instead of Lucien Rebatet! Just imagine the scandal: Schlemilovitch calls Blum a yid!' Robert was delighted at the prospect. Soon, I struck up a friendship with P.-A. Cousteau, 'the bronzed and virile Bordeaux boy', Caporal Ralph Soupault, Robert Adriveau, 'dyed-in-the-wool fascist and sentimental luminary of our dinner parties', the jolly Alain Laubreux from Toulouse and, lastly, Lucien Rebatet of the mountain infantry ('Now there's a man: he wields a pen the same way he will wield a gun when the day comes').

I immediately gave this peasant from the Dauphiné a few helpful ideas for his anti-Semitic column. From that day on, Rebatet was constantly asking for my advice. I've always thought that goys are like bulls in a china shop when it comes to understanding Jews. Even their anti-Semitism is cack-handed.

We used the same printworks as *l'Action Française*. I was dandled on Maurras' lap, stroked Pujo's beard. Maxime Real del Sarte wasn't bad either. Such delightful old men!

June 1940. I leave the merry band of *Je suis partout*, though I miss our meetings at the Place Denfert-Rochereau. I am weary of journalism and beginning to nurture political ambitions. I resolve to become a Jewish collaborator. Initially, I embark on a little high-society collaborationism: I patronise tea parties with the Propaganda-Staffel, dinners with Jean Luchaire, suppers on the Rue Lauriston, and carefully cultivate Brinon as a friend. I avoid Céline and Drieu la Rochelle, too Jewified for my taste. I quickly make myself indispensable; I am the only Jew, the 'good Jew' of the Collaborationist movement. Luchaire introduces me to Abetz. We arrange to meet. I set out my conditions: I want 1) to replace that vile little Frenchman Darquier de Pellepoix at the General Commissariat for Jewish Affairs, 2) to be given complete freedom of action. It seems to me absurd to eliminate 500,000 French Jews. Abetz seems keenly interested but does not follow up on my proposals. Nonetheless, I remain on excellent terms with him and with Stülpnagel. They advise me to contact Doriot or Déat. I don't much like Doriot because of his communist past and his braces. Déat, I see as something of a radical-socialist schoolmaster. A newcomer impresses me by his beret. I would like to say a word about Jo Darnand. Every anti-Semite has his 'good Jew': Jo Darnand is my idealised image of a good Frenchman 'with his warrior face surveying the plains'. I become his right-hand man and form solid ties with the *Milice*: the boys in navy blue have their good points, take my word for it.

Summer, 1944, after various military raids in the Vercors region, we hole up in Sigmaringen with members of the Franc-Garde. In December, during the Ardennes Offensive, I am gunned down by a GI named Lévy who looks so like me he could be my brother.

In Maurice's bookshop I found all the back-issues of *Le Gerbe*, of *Pilori* and *Je suis partout* and a few Pétainist pamphlets on the subject of training 'leaders'. Aside from pro-German literature, Maurice possesses the complete works of forgotten writers. While I read the anti-Semites Montandon and Marques-Rivière, Des Essarts becomes enthralled by the novels of Édouard Rod, Marcel Prévost, Estaunié, Boylesve, Abel Herman. He pens a brief essay: *What Is Literature?* which he dedicates to Jean-Paul Sartre.

Des Essarts is an antiquarian at heart, he intends to re-habilitate the reputations of the 1880s novelists he has just discovered. He might just as easily defend the style of Louis-Philippe or Napoleon III. The last section of his essay is entitled 'A Guide to Reading Certain Writers' and is addressed to young persons eager to improve their minds: 'Édouard Estaunié,' he writes, 'should be read in a country house at about five in the afternoon with a glass of Armagnac in hand. When reading O'Rosen or Creed, the reader should wear a formal suit, a club tie and a black silk pocket handkerchief. I recommend reading René Boylesve in summertime, in Cannes or Monte-Carlo at about eight in the evening wearing an alpaca suit. The novels of Abel Herman require sophistication: they should be read aboard a Panamanian yacht while smoking menthol cigarettes . . .'

Maurice, for his part, is writing the third tome of his memoirs: *The Revenant*, a companion volume to *The Sabbath* and *The Hunt*.

As for me, I have decided to be the greatest Jewish–French writer after Montaigne, Marcel Proust and Louis-Ferdinand Céline.

I used to have the passions and the paroxysms of a young man. Today, such naivety makes me smile. I believed that the future of Jewish literature rested on my shoulders. I looked toward the past and denounced the two-faced hypocrites: Capitaine Dreyfus, Maurois, Daniel Halévy. Proust, with his provincial childhood, was too assimilated to my mind. Edmond Fleg too nice, Benda too abstract – why play the pure spirit, Benda? The archangel of geometry? The great ascetic? The invisible Jew?

There were some beautiful lines by Spire:

Oh fervour, oh sadness, oh violence, oh madness,
Indomitable spirits to whom I am pledged,
What am I without you? Come then defend me
Against the cold, hard Reason of this happy earth . . .

And, again:

You would sing of strength, of daring,
You will love only dreamers defenceless against life
You will strive to listen to the joyous songs of peasants,
To soldiers' brutal marches, to the graceful dances of little
girls
You shall have ears only for tears . . .

Looking eastward, there are stronger personalities: Heinrich Heine, Franz Kafka . . . I loved Heine's poem 'Doña Clara': in Spain, the daughter of the Grand Inquisitor falls in love with a handsome knight who looks like Saint George. 'You have nothing in common with the vile Jews,' she tells him. The handsome knight then reveals his identity:

> *Ich, Señora, eur Geliebter,*
> *Bin der Sohn des vielbelobten,*
> *Großen, schriftgelehrten Rabbi*
> *Israel von Saragossa.* *

Much fuss was made of Franz Kafka, the elder brother of Charlie Chaplin. A few Aryan prigs put on their jackboots to trample his work: they promoted Kafka to professor of philosophy. They contrast him with the Prussian Emmanuel Kant, with the Danish genius Søren Kierkegaard, with the southerner Albert Camus, with J.-P. Sartre the half-Alsatian, half-Périgourdine penny-a-liner. I wonder how Kafka, so frail, so timid, could withstand such an onslaught.

Since becoming a naturalised Jew, Des Essarts had unreservedly embraced our cause. Maurice, on the other hand, worried about my increasing racism.

'You keep harping on at old stories,' he would say, 'it's not 1942 any more, old man! If it were, I would be strongly advising you to follow my example and join the Gestapo, that would change your perspective! People quickly forget

---

* 'I, Senora, your beloved, am the son of the learned and glorious Don Isaac Ben Israëç, Rabbi of the synagogue of Saragossa.'

their origins, you know! A little flexibility and you can change your skin at will! Change your colour! Long live the chameleon! Just watch, I can become Chinese, Apache, Norwegian, Patagonian, just like that! A quick wave of the magic wand! Abracadabra!'

I am not listening to him. I have just met Tania Arcisewska, a Polish Jew. This young woman is slowly killing herself, with no convulsions, no cries, as though it were the most obvious thing in the world. She uses a Pravaz syringe to shoot up.

'Tania exerts a baleful influence over you,' Maurice tells me. 'Why don't you find yourself a nice little Aryan girl who can sing you lullabies of the homeland?'

Tania sings me the *Prayer for the Dead of Auschwitz*. She wakes me in the middle of the night and shows me the indelible number tattooed on her shoulder.

'Look what they did to me Raphäel, look!'

She stumbles over to the window. Along the banks of the Rhône, with admirable discipline, black battalions parade and muster outside the hotel.

'Look at all the SS officers, Raphäel! See the three cops in leather coats over there on the left? It's the Gestapo, Raphaël! They're coming to the hotel! They're coming for us! They're going to gather us back to the Fatherland!'

I quickly reassure her. I have friends in high places. I have no truck with the petty pissants of the Paris *Collabo*.

I'm on first name terms with Göring; Hess, Goebbels and Heydrich consider me a friend. She's safe with me. The cops won't touch a hair on her head. If they try, I'll show them my medals; I'm the only Jew ever to be awarded the Iron Cross by Hitler himself.

One morning, taking advantage of my absence, Tania slashes her wrists. Though I was careful to hide my razor blades. Even I feel my head spin when I accidentally see those little metal objects: I feel an urge to swallow them.

The following day, an Inspector dispatched especially from Paris interrogates me. Inspecteur La Clayette, if memory serves. This woman, Tania Arcisewska, he tells me, was wanted by the police in France. Possession and trafficking of drugs. You never know what to expect with foreigners. Bloody Jews. Fucking Mittel-European delinquents. Well, anyway, she's dead and it's probably for the best.

I'm surprised by the eagerness of Inspecteur La Clayette and his keen interest in my girlfriend: former member of the Gestapo, probably.

As a memento, I kept Tania's collection of puppets: characters from the *commedia dell'arte*, Karagiozis, Pinocchio, Punchinello, the Wandering Jew, the Sleepwalker. She had placed them around her before killing herself. I think they were her only friends. Of all the puppets, my favourite is the Sleepwalker, with his arms outstretched and his eyes tight shut. Lost in her nightmare of barbed wire and watchtowers, Tania was very like him.

Then Maurice disappeared. He had always dreamed of the Orient. I can imagine him living out his retirement in Macau or Hong Kong. Maybe he's recreating his days in the Forced Labour unit on a kibbutz somewhere. I think that's the most plausible scenario.

For a week, Des Essarts and I were utterly at a loss. We no longer had the strength to concern ourselves with things of the mind and were frightened for the future: we had only sixty Swiss francs to our name. But Des Essarts' grandfather and my Venezuelan uncle Vidal drop dead the same day. Des Essarts assumes the titles of Duke and Lord; I have to make do with a vast fortune in bolivars. I was dumbfounded by my uncle Vidal's will: apparently being dandled on an old man's knee for five years is enough to make you his sole heir.

We decide to go back to France. I reassure Des Essarts: the French police are on the lookout for a Duke and Lord gone AWOL, but not for a certain Jean-François Lévy of Geneva. As soon as we cross the border, we break the bank at the casino Aix-les-Bains. I give my first press conference at the Hôtel Splendid. I'm asked what I plan to do with my bolivars: set up a harem? Build pink marble palaces? Become a patron of arts and literature? Devote myself to philanthropic works? Am I a romantic? A cynic? Will I become playboy of the year? Take the place of Rubirosa, Farouk, Ali Khan?

I will play the youthful billionaire in my own way. Obviously, I have read Larbaud and Scott Fitzgerald, but I am not about to emulate the spiritual torments of A.W. Olson Barnabooth or the puerile romanticism of Gatsby. I want to be loved for my money.

I discover I have tuberculosis and am panic-stricken. I must hide this inopportune illness which will otherwise lead to a surge in my popularity throughout the thatched cottages of Europe. Faced with a rich young man who is handsome and tubercular, little Aryan girls are apt to turn into Sainte Blandine. To discourage any such benevolence, I remind journalists that I am a Jew. Accordingly, I am drawn only to money and pleasure. People consider me photogenic: very well, I'll pull faces, wear orang-utan masks, model myself on the archetypal Jew that Aryans came to peer at in the Palais Berlitz in 1941. I evoke memories of Rabatête and Bardamu. Their insulting articles compensate me for my suffering. Sadly, no one reads these authors any more. Society journals and the romance magazines insist on showering me with praise: I am a youthful heir of great charm and originality. Jew? In the sense that Jesus Christ and Albert Einstein were Jews. So what? As a last resort I buy a yacht, *The Sanhedrin*, which I convert into a high-class brothel. I moor it off Monte Carlo, Cannes, La Baule, Deauville. From each mast, three speakers broadcast texts by Doctor Bardamu and Rabatête, my preferred PR people: Yes, through my millions and my orgies, I personally preside over the International Jewish Conspiracy. Yes, the Second World War was directly triggered by me. Yes, I am a sort of Bluebeard, a cannibal who feeds on Aryan girls though only after raping them. Yes, I dream of bankrupting the entire French peasantry and Jewifying the region of Cantal.

I quickly grow weary of these posturings. With my friend Des Essarts, I hole up in the Hôtel Trianon in Versailles to read Saint-Simon. My mother worries about my poor health. I promise to write a tragicomedy in which she will have the starring role. After that, tuberculosis can slowly carry me off. Or maybe I'll commit suicide. Thinking about it, I decide not to go out with a flourish. I would only end up being compared to L'Aiglon or Young Werther.

That evening, Des Essarts wanted me to go with him to a masked ball.

'And don't come dressed as Shylock or Süss the Jew like you always do. I've rented you a magnificent costume, you can go as Henri III. I rented a Spahi uniform for myself.'

I declined his invitation on the pretext that I had to finish my play as soon as possible. He took his leave with a sad smile. As the car was driving out of the hotel gates, I felt a pang of regret. A little later my friend killed himself on the Autoroute Ouest. An inexplicable accident. He was wearing his Spahi uniform. There was not a scratch on him.

I quickly finished my play. A tragicomedy. A tissue of invective against *goyim*. I felt sure it would rile Parisian audiences; they would never forgive me for flaunting my neuroses and my racism on stage in such a provocative manner. I set much store by the virtuoso finale: in a white-walled room, father and son clash; the son is wearing a threadbare SS uniform and a tattered Gestapo trench coat, the father a skullcap, sidelocks and a rabbi's beard. They parody an interrogation scene, the son playing the role of the torturer, the father the role of the victim. The mother bursts into the room and rushes at them, arms outstretched, eyes wild. She wails the 'Ballad of Marie Sanders, the "Jews' Whore"'. The son grabs his father by the throat and launches into the 'Horst-Wessel-Lied' but cannot drown out his mother's voice. The father, half choking, mewls the 'Kol Nidrei', the great Prayer of Atonement. Suddenly, a door at the back of the stage is flung open: four nurses circle the protagonists and, with difficulty, overpower them. The curtain falls. No one applauds. People stare at me suspiciously. They had expected better manners from a Jew. I'm an ungrateful wretch. A boor. I have appropriated their clear and limpid language and transformed it into a hysterical cacophony.

They had hoped to discover a new Proust, a rough-hewn Yid polished by contact with their culture, they came expecting sweet music only to be deafened by ominous tom-toms. Now they know where they stand with me. I can die happy.

I was terribly disappointed by the reviews the following morning. They were patronising. I had to face facts. I would meet with no hostility from my peers, excepting the occasional Lady Bountiful and old men who looked like Colonel de la Rocque. The newspapers spent even more column inches concerned with my state of mind. The French have an overweening affection for whores who write memoirs, pederast poets, Arab pimps, Negro junkies and Jewish provocateurs. Clearly, there was no morality any more. The Jew was a prized commodity, we were overly respected. I could graduate from Saint-Cyr and become Maréchal Schlemilovitch: there would be no repeat of the Dreyfus Affair.

After this fiasco, all that was left was for me to disappear like Maurice Sachs. To leave Paris for good. I bequeathed a part of my inheritance to my mother. I remembered that I had a father in America. I suggested he might like to visit me if he wanted to inherit 350,000 dollars. The answer came by return of post: he arranged to meet me in Paris at the Hôtel Continental. I was keen to pamper my tuberculosis. To become a prudent, polite young man. A real little Aryan. The problem was I didn't like sanatoriums. I preferred to travel. My woppish soul longed for beautiful, exotic locations.

I felt that the French provinces would provide these more effectively than Mexico or the Sunda Islands. And so

I turned my back on my cosmopolitan past. I was keen to get to know the land, with paraffin lamps, and the song of the thickets and the forests.

And then I thought about my mother, who frequently toured the provinces. The Karinthy Theatre Company, light comedy guaranteed. Since she spoke French with a Balkan accent, she played Russian princesses, Polish countesses and Hungarian horsewomen. Princess Berezovo in Aurillac. Countess Tomazoff in Béziers. Baronne Gevatchaldy in Saint-Brieuc. The Karinthy Theatre Company tours all over France.

II

My father was wearing an *eau de Nil* suit, a green-striped shirt, a red tie and astrakhan shoes. I had just made his acquaintance in the Ottoman Lounge of the Hôtel Continental. Having signed various papers making over a part of my fortune to him, I said:

'In short, your New York business ventures are a dismal flop? What were you thinking, becoming chairman and managing director of Kaleidoscope Ltd? You should have noticed that the kaleidoscope market is falling by the day! Children prefer space rockets, electromagnetism, arithmetic! Dreams aren't selling any more, old man. And let me be frank, you're a Jew, which means you have no head for commerce or for business. Leave that honour to the French. If you knew how to read, I would show you the elegant comparison I drew up between Peugeot and Citroën: on the one hand, a provincial man from Montbéliard, miserly, discreet, prosperous; on the other, André Citroën, a tragic Jewish adventurer who gambles for high stakes in casinos. Come, come, you don't have the makings of a captain of industry. This is all an act! You're a tightrope walker, nothing more! There's no point putting on an act, making feverish telephone calls to Madagascar, to Liechtenstein, to Tierra del Fuego! You'll never offload your stock of kaleidoscopes.'

My father wanted to visit Paris, where he had spent his youth. We had a couple of gin fizzes at Fouquet's, at the Relais Plaza, at the bars of Le Meurice, the Saint James Albany, the Élysée-Park, the Georges V, the Lancaster. This was his version of the provinces. While he puffed on a Partagas cigar, I was thinking about Touraine and the forest of Brocéliande. Where would I choose to live out my exile? Tours? Nevers? Poitiers? Aurillac? Pézenas? La Souterraine? Everything I knew of the French provinces I had learned from the pages of the *Guide Michelin* and various authors such as François Mauriac.

I had been particularly moved by a text by this writer from the Landes: *Bordeaux, of Adolescence*. I remember Mauriac's surprise when I passionately recited his beautiful prose: 'That town in which we were born, in which we were a child, an adolescent, is the only one we must forbear to judge. It is part of us, it is ourselves, we carry it within us. The history of Bordeaux is the history of my body and my soul.' Did my old friend understand that I envied him his adolescence, the Marianist Brothers school, the Place des Quinconces, the scents of balmy heather, of warm sand, of resin? What adolescence could I, Raphäel Schlemilovitch, recount other than that of miserable little stateless Jew? I would not be Gérard de Nerval, nor François Mauriac, nor even Marcel Proust. I had no Valois to stir my soul, no Guyenne, no Combray. I had no Tante Léonie. Doomed to Fouquet's, to the Relais Plaza, to the Élysée-Park where I drink disgusting English liqueurs in the company of a fat New York Jew: my father. Alcohol fosters a need in him to confide, as it had Maurice Sachs on the day we first met. Their fates are the same with one small difference: Sachs read Saint-Simon, while my father read Maurice Dekobra. Born in Caracas to a Sephardic Jewish family, he hurriedly fled the Americas to escape the police of the dictator of the Galapagos islands whose daughter he had seduced. In France, he became secretary to Stavinsky. In those days, he looked very dapper: somewhere between Valentino and Novarro with a touch of Douglas Fairbanks, enough to turn the heads of pretty Aryan girls. Ten years later his photograph was among those at the anti-Jewish exhibition at the Palais Berlitz, accompanied by the caption: 'Devious Jew. He could pass for a South American.'

My father was not without a certain sense of humour: one afternoon, he went to the Palais Berlitz and offered to act as a guide for several visitors to the exhibition. When they came to the photo, he cried: 'Peek-a-boo! Here I am!' The Jewish penchant for showing off cannot be overstated. In fact, my father had a certain sympathy for the Germans since they patronised his favourite haunts: the Continental, the Majestic, Le Meurice. He lost no opportunity to rub shoulders with them in Maxim's, Philippe, Gaffner, Lola Tosch and other nightclubs thanks to false papers in the name Jean Cassis de Coudray-Macouard.

He lived in a tiny garret room on the Rue des Saussaies directly opposite the Gestapo. Late into the night he would sit up reading *Bagatelles pour un massacre*, which he found very funny. To my stupefaction, he could recite whole pages from the book. He had bought it because of the title, thinking it was a crime novel.

In July 1944, he managed to sell Fontainebleau forest to the Germans using a Baltic baron as a middleman. With the profits of this delicate operation, he emigrated to the United States where he set up the company Kaleidoscope Ltd.

'What about you?' he asked, blowing a cloud of Partagas smoke into my face. 'Tell me about your life.'

'Haven't you been reading the papers?' I said wearily. 'I thought *Confidential* magazine in New York devoted a special issue to me? Basically, I've decided to give up this shallow, decadent cosmopolitan life. I'm retiring to the provinces, the French countryside, back to the land. I've just settled on Bordeaux, the Guyenne, as a rest cure for my nerves. It's also a little homage to an old friend, François Mauriac. I'm guessing the name means nothing to you?'

We had one for the road in the bar at the Ritz.

'May I accompany you to this city you mentioned earlier?' he asked out of the blue. 'You're my son, we should at least take a trip together. And besides, thanks to you, I'm now the fourth-richest man in America!'

'By all means come along if you like. After that, you can go back to New York.'

He kissed me on the forehead and I felt tears come to my eyes. This fat man with his motley clothes was genuinely moving.

Arm in arm, we crossed the Place Vendôme. My father sang snatches of *Bagatelles pour un massacre* in a fine bass voice. I was thinking about the terrible things I had read during my childhood. Particularly the series *How to kill your father* by André Breton and Jean-Paul Sartre (the 'Read Me' series for boys). Breton advised boys to station themselves at the window of their house on the Avenue Foch and slaughter the first passing pedestrian. This man necessarily being their father, a *préfet de police* or a textile manufacturer. Sartre temporarily forsook the well-heeled *arrondissements* for the Communist-controlled suburbs of the *banlieue rouge*: here, middle-class boys were urged to approach the brawniest labourers, apologise for being bourgeois brats, drag them back to the Avenue Foch where they would smash the Sèvres china, kill the father, at which point the young man would politely ask to be raped. This latter method, while exhibiting greater perversity, the rape following the murder, was also more grandiose: the proletariat of all countries were being called upon to settle a family spat. It was recommended that young men insult their father before killing him. Some who made a name for themselves in such literature developed charming expressions. For example: 'Families, I despise you' (the son of a French pastor). 'I'll fight the next war in a German uniform.' 'I shit upon the French army' (the son of a French *préfet de police*). 'You are a BASTARD' (the son of a French naval officer). I gripped my father's arm more tightly. There was nothing to distinguish between us. Isn't that right, my podgy papa? How could I kill you? I love you.

We caught the Paris–Bordeaux train. From the window of the compartment, France looked particularly splendid. Orléans, Beaugency, Vendôme, Tours, Poitiers, Angoulême. My father was no longer wearing a pale green suit, a pink buckskin tie, a tartan shirt, a platinum signet ring and the shoes with the astrakhan spats. I was no longer called Raphäel Schlemilovitch.

I was the eldest son of a notary from Libourne and we were heading back to our home in the country. While a certain Raphäel Schlemilovitch was squandering his youth in Cap Ferrat, in Monte Carlo and in Paris, my obdurate neck was bowed over Latin translations. Over and over, I repeated to myself 'Rue d'Ulm! Rue d'Ulm!' feeling my cheeks flush. In June I would pass the entrance exam to the École Normale Supérieure. I would definitively 'go up' to Paris. On the Rue d'Ulm, I would share rooms with a young provincial lad like myself. An unshakeable friendship would develop between us. We would be Jallez and Jephanion. One night, we would climb the steps of the Butte Montmartre. We would see Paris laid out at our feet. In a soft, resolute voice we would say: 'Now, Paris, it's just you and me!' We would write beautiful letters to our families: 'Maman, I love you, your little man.' At night, in the silence of our rooms, we would talk about our future mistresses: the Jewish baronesses, the daughters of captains of industry, actresses, courtesans. They would admire our brilliance and our expertise. One afternoon, hearts pounding, we would knock on the door of Gaston Gallimard: 'We're students at the École Normale Supérieure, monsieur, and we wanted to show you our first essays.' Later, the Collège de France, a career in politics, a panoply of honours. We would be part of our country's elite. Our brains would be in Paris but our hearts would ever remain in the provinces. In the maelstrom of the capital, we would think fondly of our native Cantal, our native Gironde. Every year, we would go back to clear out our lungs and visit our parents somewhere near Saint-Flour or Libourne. We would leave again weighted down with cheeses and bottles of Saint-Émilion. Our mamans would have knitted us thick cardigans: the winters in Paris are cold. Our sisters would marry pharmacists from Aurillac and insurance brokers from Bordeaux. We would serve as examples to our nephews.

Gare Saint-Jean, night is waiting for us. We have seen nothing of Bordeaux. In the taxi to the Hôtel Splendid, I whisper to my father:

'The driver is definitely a member of the French Gestapo, my plump papa.'

'You think so?', my father says, playing along. 'That could prove awkward. I forgot to bring the fake papers in the name Coudray-Macouard.'

'I suspect he's taking us to the Rue Lauriston to visit his friends Bonny and Lafont.'

'I think you're wrong: I think he's heading for the Gestapo headquarters on Avenue Foch.'

'Maybe Rue des Saussaies for an identity check?'

'The first red light we come to, we make a run for it.'

'Impossible, the doors are locked.'

'What then?'

'Wait it out. Keep your chin up.'

'We could probably pass for Jewish collaborators. Sell them Fontainebleau forest at a bargain price. I'll tell them I worked at *Je suis partout* before the war. A quick phone call to Brasillach or Laubreux or Rebatet and we're home free . . .'

'You think they'll let us make a phone call?'

'It doesn't matter. We'll sign up to join the LVF or the *Milice*, show a little goodwill. In a green uniform and an alpine beret we can make it to the Spanish border. After that . . .'

'Freedom . . .'

'Shh! He's listening . . .'

'He looks like Darnand, don't you think?'

'If it is him, we've really got problems. The *Milice* are bound to give us a tough time.'

'I don't like to say, but I think I was right . . . we're taking the motorway heading west . . . the headquarters of the *Milice* is in Versailles . . . We're really in the shit!'

At the hotel bar, we sat drinking Irish coffee, my father was smoking his Upmann cigar. How did the Splendid differ from the Claridge, from the Georges V, and every other caravanserai in Paris and Europe? How much longer can grand hotels and Pullman cars protect me from France? When all is said and done, these gold-fish bowls made me sick. But the resolutions I had made gave me a little hope. I would sign up to study *lettres supérieures* at the Lycée de Bordeaux. When I passed my entrance exam, I would be careful not to sign Rastignac, from the heights of the Butte Montmartre. I had nothing in common with this gallant little Frenchman. 'Now, Paris, it's just you and me!' Only paymasters from Saint-Flour or Libourne could be so starry-eyed. No, Paris was too much like me. An artificial flower in the middle of France. I was counting on Bordeaux to teach me true values, to put me in touch with the land. After I graduated, I would apply for a post as a provincial schoolteacher. I would divide my days between a dusty classroom and the Café du Commerce. I would play cards with colonels. On Sunday afternoons, I would listen to old mazurkas from the bandstand in the town square. I would fall in love with the mayor's wife, we'd meet on Thursdays in a *hôtel de passe* in the next town. It would all depend on the nearest country town. I would serve France by educating her children. I would belong to the battalion of the 'black hussars' of truth, to quote Péguy, whom I could count among my colleagues. Gradually I would forget my shameful origins, the dishonourable name Schlemilovitch, Torquemada, Himmler and so many other things.

Rue Sainte-Catherine, people turned as we passed. Probably because of my father's purple suit, his Kentucky green shirt and the same old shoes with the astrakhan spats. I fondly wished a policeman would stop us. I would have justified myself once and for all to the French, tirelessly explaining that for twenty years we had been corrupted by one of their own, a man from Alsace. He insisted that the Jew would not exist if goys did not condescend to notice him. And so we are forced to attract *their* attention by wearing garish clothes. For us, as Jews, it is a matter of life and death.

The headmaster of the lycée invited us into his office. He seemed to doubt whether the son of this dago could genuinely want to study *lettres supérieures*. His own son – *Monsieur le proviseur* was proud of his son – had spent the holidays tirelessly swotting up on his *Maquet-et-Roger**. I felt like telling the headmaster that, alas, I was a Jew. Hence: always top of the class.

The headmaster handed me an anthology of Greek orators and told me to open the book at random. I had to gloss a passage by Aeschines. I acquitted myself brilliantly. I went so far as to translate the text into Latin.

The headmaster was dumbfounded. Was he really ignorant of the keenness, the intelligence of Jews? Had he really forgotten the great writers we had given France: Montaigne, Racine, Saint-Simon, Sartre, Henry Bordeaux, René Bazin, Proust, Louis-Ferdinand Céline . . . On the spot, he suggested I skip the first year and enrolled me straight into the second year – *khâgne*.

---

* Latin grammar

'Congratulations, Schlemilovitch,' he said, his voice quavering with emotion.

After we had left the lycée, I rebuked my father for his obsequiousness, his Turkish Delight unctuousness in dealing with the *proviseur*.

'What are you thinking, playing Mata Hari in the office of a French bureaucrat? I could excuse your doe eyes and your obsequiousness if it was an SS executioner you were trying to charm! But doing your belly dance in front of that good man! He was hardly going to eat you, for Christ's sake! Here, I'll make you suffer!'

I broke into a run. He followed me as far as Tourny, he did not even ask me to stop. When he was out of breath, he probably thought I would take advantage of his tiredness and give him the slip forever. He said:

'A bracing little run is good for the heart . . . It'll give us an appetite . . .'

He didn't even stand up for himself. He was trying to outwit his sadness, trying to tame it. Something he learned in the pogroms, probably. My father mopped his forehead with his pink buckskin tie. How could he think I would desert him, leave him alone, helpless in this city of distinguished tradition, in this illustrious night that smelled of vintage wine and English tobacco? I took him by the arm. He was a whipped cur.

Midnight. I open the bedroom window a crack. The summer air, 'Stranger on the shore', drifts up to us. My father says:

'There must be a nightclub around here somewhere.'

'I didn't come to Bordeaux to play the lothario. And anyway, you can expect meagre pickings: two or three degenerate kids from the Bordeaux bourgeoisie, a couple of English tourists . . .'

He slips on a sky-blue dinner jacket. I knot a tie from Sulka in front of the mirror. We plunge into the warm sickly waters, a South American band plays rumbas. We sit at a table, my father orders a bottle of Pommery, lights an Upmann cigar. I buy a drink for an English girl with dark hair and green eyes. Her face reminds me of something. She smells deliciously of cognac. I hold her to me. Suddenly, slimy hotel names come tumbling from her lips: Eden Rock, Rampoldi, Balmoral, Hôtel de Paris: we had met in Monte Carlo. I glance over the English girl's shoulder at my father. He smiles and makes conspiratorial gestures. He's touching, he probably wants me to marry some Slavo-Argentinian heiress, but ever since I arrived in Bordeaux, I have been in love with the Blessed Virgin, with Joan of Arc and Eleanor of Aquitaine. I try to explain this until three in the morning but he chain-smokes his cigars and does not listen. We have had too much to drink.

We fell asleep at dawn. The streets of Bordeaux were teeming with cars mounted with loudspeakers: 'Operation rat extermination campaign, operation rat extermination campaign. For you, free rat poison, just ask at this car.

Citizens of Bordeaux, operation rat extermination . . . operation rat extermination . . .'

We walk through the streets of the city, my father and I. Cars appear from all sides, hurtling straight for us, their sirens wailing. We hide in doorways. We were huge American rats.

In the end we had to part ways. On the evening before term started, I tossed my clothes in a heap in the middle of the room: ties from Sulka and the Via Condotti, cashmere sweaters, Doucet scarves, suits from Creed, Canette, Bruce O'lofson, O'Rosen, pyjamas from Lanvin, handkerchiefs from Henri à la Pensée, belts by Gucci, shoes by Dowie & Marshall . . .

'Here,' I said to my father, 'you can take all this back to New York – a souvenir of your son. From now on the *khâgne* scholar's beret and the ash-grey smock will protect me from myself. I'm giving up smoking Craven and Khédive. From now on it's shag tobacco. I've become a naturalised Frenchman. I'm definitively assimilated. Will I join the category of military Jews, like Dreyfus and Stroheim? We'll see. But right now, I am studying to apply to the *École Normale Supérieure* like Blum, Fleg and Henri Franck. It would have been tactless to apply to the military academy at Saint-Cyr straightaway.'

We had a last gin fizz at the bar of the Splendid. My father was wearing his travelling outfit: a crimson fur cap, an astrakhan coat and blue crocodile-skin shoes. A Partagas cigar dangled from his lips. Dark glasses concealed his eyes. He was crying, I realised, from the quaver in his voice. He was so overcome he forgot the language of this country and mumbled a few words in English.

'You'll come and visit me in New York?' he asked.

'I don't think so, old man. I'm going to die before very long. I've just got time to pass the entrance exam to the *École Normale Supérieure*, the first stage of assimilation. I promise you your grandson will be a Maréchal de France. Oh, yes, I am planning to try and reproduce.'

On the station platform, I said:

'Don't forget to send me a postcard from New York or Acapulco.'

He hugged me. As the train pulled out, my Guyenne plans seemed suddenly laughable. Why had I not followed this unhoped-for partner in crime? Together, we would have outshone the Marx Brothers. We ad-lib grotesque maudlin gags for the public. Schlemilovitch *père* is a tubby man dressed in garish multi-coloured suits. The children are thrilled by these two clowns. Especially when Schlemilovitch junior trips Schlemilovitch *père* who falls head-first into a vat of tar. Or when Schlemilovitch *fils* rips away a ladder and sends Schlemilovitch *père* tumbling. Or when Schlemilovitch *fils* surreptitiously sets fire to Schlemilovitch *père*, etc.

They are currently performing at the Cirque Médrano, following a sell-out tour of Germany. Schlemilovitch *père* and Schlemilovitch *fils* are true Parisian stars, though they shun elite audiences in favour of local cinemas and provincial circuses.

I bitterly regretted my father's departure. For me, adulthood had begun. There was only one boxer left in the ring. He was punching himself. Soon he would black out. In the meantime, would I have the chance – if only for a minute – to catch the public's attention?

It was raining, as it does every Sunday before term starts. The cafés were glittering more brightly than usual. On the way to the lycée, I felt terribly presumptuous: a frivolous young Jew cannot suddenly aspire to the dogged tenacity conferred upon scholarship students by their patrician ancestry. I remembered what my old friend Seingalt had written in chapter II of volume III of his memoirs: 'A new career was opening before me. Fortune was still my friend, and I had all the necessary qualities to second the efforts of the blind goddess on my behalf save one – perseverance.' Could I really become a *normalien*?

Fleg, Blum and Henri Franck must have had a drop of Breton blood.

I went up to the dormitory. I had had no experience of secular schooling since Hattemer (the Swiss boarding schools in which my mother enrolled me were run by Jesuits). I was shocked, therefore, to find there were no prayers. I conveyed my concerns to the other boarders. They burst out laughing, mocked the Blessed Virgin and then suggested I shine their shoes on the pretext that they had been there longer than I.

My objection was twofold:

1) I could not understand why they had no respect for the Blessed Virgin.

2) I had no doubt that they had been here 'before me', since Jewish immigration to the Bordeaux area did not begin until the fifteenth century. I was a Jew. They were Gauls. They were persecuting me.

Two boys stepped forward to arbitrate. A Christian Democrat and a Bordeaux Jew. The former whispered to me that he didn't want too much talk of the Blessed Virgin because he was hoping to forge ties with students on the extreme left. The latter accused me of being an 'agent provocateur'. Besides, the Jew didn't really exist, he was an Aryan invention, etc., etc.

I explained to the former that the Blessed Virgin was surely worthy of a falling out with anyone and everyone. I informed him of how strongly Saint John of the Cross and Pascal would have condemned his toadying Catholicism. I added that, moreover, as a Jew it was not my place to give him catechism lessons.

The comments of the latter filled me with a profound sadness: the goys had done a fine job of brainwashing.

I had been warned; thereafter they completely ostracised me.

Adrien Debigorre, who taught us French literature and language, had an imposing beard, a black frock-coat, and a club foot that elicited mocking comments from the students. This curious character had been a friend of Maurras, of Paul Chack and Monsignor Mayol de Lupé; French radio listeners will probably remember the 'Fireside chats' Debigorre gave on Radio-Vichy.

In 1942, Debigorre is part of the inner circle of Abel Bonheur, the Ministre de l'Éducation nationale. He is indignant when Bonheur, dressed as Anne de Bretagne, declares in a soft tremulous tone: 'If we had a princess in France, we should push her into the arms of Hitler', or when the minister praised the 'manly charms' of the SS. Eventually he fell out with Bonheur, nicknaming him *la Gestapette*, something Pétain found hilarious. Retiring to the Minquier islands, Debigorre tried to organise commandos of local fishermen to mount a resistance against the British. His Anglophobia rivalled that of Henri Béraud. As a child he had solemnly promised his father, a naval lieutenant from Saint-Malo, that he would never forget the 'TRICK' of Trafalgar. During the attack on Mers-el-Kébir, he is said to have thundered: 'They will pay for this!' During the war, he kept up a voluminous correspondence with Paul Chack and would read us passages from their letters. My classmates missed no opportunity to humiliate him. At the beginning of class, he would stand up and sing 'Maréchal, nous voilà!' The blackboard was covered with *francisques* and photographs of Pétain. Debigorre would talk but no one paid him any heed. Sometimes, he would bury his head in his hands and sob. One student, a colonel's son named Gerbier, would shout 'Adrien's blubbing!' The whole class would roar with laughter. Except me, of course. I decided to be the poor man's bodyguard. Despite my recent bout of tuberculosis, I stood six foot six and weighed nearly 200 pounds, and as luck would have it, I had been born in a country of short-arsed bastards.

I began by splitting Gerbier's eyebrow. A lawyer's son, a boy named Val-Suzon, called me a 'Nazi'. I broke three of his vertebrae in memory of SS officer Schlemilovitch who died on the Russian front during the Ardennes Offensive. All that remained was to bring a few little Gauls to heel: Chatel-Gérard, Saint-Thibault, La Rochepot. Thereafter it was I and not Debigorre who read Maurras, Chack or Béraud at the beginning of class. Terrified of my vicious streak, you could hear a pin drop, this was the reign of Jewish terror and our old schoolmaster soon found his smile again.

After all, why did classmates make such a show of seeming disgusted?

Surely Maurras, Chack and Béraud were just like their grandfathers.

Here I was taking the trouble to introduce them to the healthiest, the purest of their compatriots and the ungrateful bastards called me a 'Nazi' . . .

'Let's have them study the *Romanciers du terroir*,' I suggested to Debigorre. 'These little degenerates need to study the rural novels celebrating their fathers' glories. It'll make a change from Trotsky, Kafka and the rest of that gypsy rabble. Besides, it's not like they even understand them. It takes two thousand years of pogroms, my dear Debigorre, to be able to tackle such books. If I were called Val-Suzon, I wouldn't be so presumptuous. I'd settle for exploring the provinces, quenching my thirst from French springs! Listen, for the first term, we'll teach them about your friend Béraud. A good solid writer from Lyons seems entirely appropriate. A few comments on novels like *Les Lurons de Sabolas* . . . We can follow up with Eugène le Roy: *Jacquou le Croquant* and *Mademoiselle de la Ralphie* will teach them the beauties of the Périgord. A little detour through Quercy courtesy of Léon Cladel. A trip to Bretagne under the aegis of Charles Le Goffic. Roupnel can take us on a tour of Bourgogne. The Bourbonnais will hold no secrets for us after reading Guillaumin's *La Vie d'un simple*. Through Alphonse Daudet and Paul Arène we will smell the scents of Provence. We can discuss Maurras and Mistral! In the second term, we can revel in the Touraine autumn with René Boylesve. Have you read *L'Enfant à la balustrade*? It's remarkable! The third term will be devoted to the psychological novels of the Dijon author Édouard Estaunié. In short, a sentimental tour of France! What do you think of my syllabus?'

Debigorre was smiling and clasping my hands in his. He said to me:

'Schlemilovitch, you are a scholar and patriot! If only the native French lads were like you!'

Debigorre often invites me to his home. He lives in a room cluttered with books and papers. On the walls hang yellowing photographs of various oddballs: Bichelonne, Hérold-Paquis and admirals Esteva, Darlan and Platón. His elderly housekeeper serves us tea. At about 11 p.m. we have an aperitif on the terrace of the Café de Bordeaux. On my first visit, I surprise him hugely by talking about Maurras' mannerisms and Pujo's beard. 'But you weren't even born, Raphäel!' Debigorre thinks it is a case of transmigration of souls, that in some former life I was a fierce supporter of Maurras, a pure-blood Frenchman, an unrepentant Gaulois and a Jewish collaborator to boot: 'Ah, Raphäel, how I wish you had been in Bordeaux in June 1940! Picture the outrageous scenes! Gentlemen with beards and black frockcoats! University students! Ministers of the RÉ-PU-BLI-QUE are chattering away! Making grand gestures! Réda Caire and Maurice Chevalier are singing songs! Suddenly – BANG! – blond bare-chested youths burst into the Café du Commerce! They start a wholesale massacre! The gentlemen in frockcoats are thrown against the ceiling. They slam into the walls, crash into the rows of bottles. They splash about in puddles of Pernod, heads slashed by broken glass! The manageress, a woman named Marianne, is running this way and that. She gives little cries. The woman's an old whore! THE SLUT! Her skirt falls off. She's gunned down in a hail of machine-gun fire. Caire and Chevalier suddenly fall silent. What a sight, Raphäel, for enlightened minds like ours! What vengeance! . . . '

Eventually, I tire of my role as martinet. Since my classmates refuse to accept that Maurras, Chack and Béraud are their people, since they look down on Charles Le Goffic and Paul Arène, Debigorre and I will talk to them about some more universal aspects of 'French genius': vividness and ribaldry, the beauties of classicism, the pertinence of moralists, the irony of Voltaire, the subtleties of psychological novels, the heroic tradition from Corneille to Georges Bernanos. Debigorre bridles at the mention of Voltaire. I am equally repulsed by that bourgeois 'rebel' and anti-Semite, but if we don't mention him in our *Panorama of French genius*, we will be accused of bias. 'Let's be reasonable,' I say to Debigorre, 'you know perfectly well that I personally prefer Joseph de Maistre. Let's make a little effort to include Voltaire.'

Once again, Saint-Thibault disrupts one of our lectures. An inopportune remark by Debigorre, 'The utterly French grace of the exquisite Mme de La Fayette', has my classmate leaping from his seat in indignation.

'When are you going to stop talking about "French genius", about how something is "quintessentially French", about "the French tradition"?' bellows the young Gaulois. My mentor Trotsky says that the Revolution knows no country . . .

'My dear Saint-Thibault,' I said, 'you're starting to get on my nerves. You are too jowly and your blood too thick for the name Trotsky from your lips to be anything other than blasphemy. My dear Saint-Thibault, your great-great-uncle Charles Maurras wrote that it is impossible to understand Mme de La Fayette or Chamfort unless one has tilled the soil of France for a thousand years! Now it is my turn to tell you something, my dear Saint-Thibault: it takes a thousand years of pogroms, of auto-da-fés and ghettos to understand even a paragraph of Marx or Bronstein . . . BRONSTEIN, my dear Saint-Thibault, and not Trotsky as you so elegantly call him! Now shut your trap, my dear Saint-Thibault, or I shall . . .'

The parents' association were up in arms, the headmaster summoned me to his office.

'Schlemilovitch,' he told me, 'Messieurs Gerbier, Val-Suzon and La Rochepot have filed a complaint charging you with assault and battery of their sons. Defending your schoolmaster is all very commendable but you have been behaving like a lout. Do you realise that Val-Suzon has been hospitalised? That Gerbier and

La Rochepot have suffered audio-visual disturbances? These are elite *khâgne* students! You could go to prison, Schlemilovitch, to prison! But for now you will leave this school, this very evening!'

'If these gentlemen want to press charges,' I said, 'I am prepared to defend myself once and for all. I'll get a lot of publicity. Paris is not Bordeaux, you know. In Paris, they always side with the poor little Jew, not with the brutish Aryans! I'll play the persecuted martyr to perfection. The Left will organise rallies and demonstrations and, believe me, it will be the done thing to sign a petition in support of Raphäel Schlemilovitch. All in all, the scandal will do considerable damage to your prospects for promotion. Remember Capitaine Dreyfus and, much more recently, all the fuss about Jacob X, the young Jewish deserter . . . Parisians are crazy about us. They always side with us. Forgive us anything. Wipe the slate clean. What do you expect? Moral standards have gone to hell since the last war – what am I saying? Since the Middle Ages! Remember the wonderful French custom where every Easter the Comte de Toulouse would ceremoniously slap the head of the Jewish community, while the man begged "Again, *monsieur le comte*! One more, with the pommel of your sword! Batter me! Rip out my guts! Trample my corpse!" A blessed age. How could my forebear from Toulouse ever imagine that one day I would break Val-Suzon's vertebrae? Put out the eye of a Gerbier or a La Rochepot? Every dog has his day, headmaster. Revenge is a dish best served cold. And don't think even for a minute that I feel remorse. You can tell the young men's parents that I'm sorry I didn't slaughter them. Just imagine the trial. A young Jew, pale and passionate, declaring that he sought only to avenge the beatings regularly meted out to his ancestors by the Comte de Toulouse! Sartre would defend me, it would take centuries off him! I'd be carried in triumph from the Place de l'Étoile to the Bastille! I'd be a fucking prince to the young people of France!'

'You are loathsome, Schlemilovitch, LOATHSOME! I refuse to listen to you a moment longer.'

'That's right, *monsieur le proviseur*, loathsome!'

'I am calling the police this instant!'

'Oh, surely not the police, *monsieur le proviseur*, call the Gestapo, please.'

I left the lycée for good. Debigorre was upset to lose his finest pupil. We met up two or three times at the Café de Bordeaux. One Sunday evening, he did not appear. His housekeeper told me he had been taken to a mental home in Arcachon. I was strictly forbidden from seeing him. Only monthly visits from family members were permitted.

I knew that every night my former teacher was calling out to me for help because apparently Léon Blum was hounding him with implacable hatred. Via his house-keeper, he sent me a hastily scrawled message: 'Save me, Raphäel. Blum and the others are trying to kill me. I'm sure of it. They slip into my room like reptiles in the night. They taunt me. They threaten me with butcher's knives. Blum, Mandel, Zay, Salengro, Dreyfus and the rest of them. They want to hack me to pieces. I'm begging you, Raphäel, save me.'

That was the last I heard of him.

O ld men, it would seem, play a crucial role in my life.

Two weeks after leaving the lycée, I was spending my last few francs at the Restaurant Dubern when a man sat down at the table next to mine. My attention was immediately drawn to his monocle and his long jade cigarette holder. He was completely bald, which gave him a rather unsettling appearance. As he ate, he never took his eyes off me. He beckoned the head waiter with an insolent flick of the finger: his index seemed to trace an arabesque in the air. I saw him write a few words on a visiting card. He pointed to me and the head waiter brought over the little white rectangle on which I read:

VICOMTE CHARLES LÉVY-VENDÔME
Master of Ceremonies, would like the pleasure of your acquaintance

He takes a seat opposite me.

'Excuse my rather cavalier manner, but I invariably force an entry into other people's lives. A face, an expression, can be enough to win my friendship. I was most impressed by your resemblance to Gregory Peck. Aside from that, what do you do for a living?'

He had a beautiful, deep voice.

'You can tell me your life story somewhere more dusky. What do you say to the Morocco?'

At the Morocco, the dance floor was utterly deserted despite Noro Morales' wild *guarachas* blasting from the loudspeakers. Latin America was decidedly the vogue in Bordeaux that autumn.

'I've just been expelled from school,' I explained, 'aggravated assault. I'm a young hoodlum, and Jewish to boot. My name is Raphäel Schlemilovitch.'

'Schlemilovitch? Well, well! All the more reason that we should be friends. I myself belong to a long-established Jewish family from the Loiret. My ancestors were jesters to the dukes of Pithiviers for generations. Your life story does not interest me. I wish to know whether or not you are looking for work.'

'I am looking, *monsieur le vicomte*.'

'Very well then. I am a host. I host . . . I conceive, I develop, I devise . . . I have need of your help. You are a young man of impeccable pedigree. Good presence, come-hither eyes,

American smile. Let us speak man to man. What do you think of French girls?'

'Pretty.'

'And?'

'They would make first-class whores!'

'Admirable! I like your turn of phrase! Now, cards on table, Schlemilovitch! I work in the white slave trade! As it happens, the French girl is particularly prized in the market. You will supply the merchandise. I am too old to take on such work. In 1925, it required no effort; these days, if I wish to be attractive to women, I have them smoke opium beforehand. Who would have thought the sultry young Lévy-Vendôme would turn into a satyr when he turned fifty? Now, you Schlemilovitch, you have many years ahead of you; make the most of them! Use your natural talents to debauch your Aryan girls. Later, you can write your memoir. It will be called *The Rootless*: *the story of seven French girls who could not resist the charms of Schlemilovitch the Jew only to find themselves, one fine day, working in brothels in the Orient or in South America*. The moral of the story: they should not have trusted this Jewish lothario, they should have stayed on the cool mountain slopes, in the verdant groves. You will dedicate your memoir to Maurice Barrès.'

'As you wish, *monsieur le vicomte*.'

'Now, to work, my boy. You leave immediately for the Haute-Savoie. I have just received an order from Rio de

Janeiro: "Young French mountain girl. Brunette. Husky."
From there, you will move on to Normandy. This time
the order is from Beirut: "Elegant French girl whose
ancestors fought in the crusades. Good provincial landed
gentry." The client is clearly a lecher after our own
hearts! An emir who wants to avenge himself for Charles
Martel . . .'

'Or the sack of Constantinople by the crusaders . . .'

'If you prefer. In short, I have found what he requires.
In the Calvados region . . . A young woman . . . descended
from a venerable aristocratic family! Seventeenth-century
château! Cross and Lance heads with fleurs-de-lis on a
field Azure. Hunting parties! The ball is in your court,
Schlemilovitch. There is not a moment to lose. We have
our work cut out for us! The abductions must involve no
bloodshed. Come, have one last drink at my place, then I
will accompany you to the station.'

Lévy-Vendôme's apartment is furnished in the
Napoleon III style. The vicomte ushers me into his library.

'Have you ever seen such exquisite bindings?' he says,
'I am a bibliophile, it is my secret vice. See, if I take down
a volume at random: a treatise on aphrodisiacs by René
Descartes. Apocrypha, nothing but apocrypha . . . I have
single-handedly reinvented the whole history of French
literature. Here we have the love letters of Pascal to Mlle
de La Vallière. A bawdy saga by Boussuet. An erotic tale
by Mme de La Fayette. Not content with debauching the

women of this country, I wanted to prostitute French literature in its entirety. To transform the heroines of Racine and Marivaux into whores. Junia willingly copulating with Nero as a horrified Britannicus looks on. Andromache throwing herself into the arms of Pyrrhus at their first meeting. Marivaux's countesses donning their maids' uniforms and "borrowing" their lovers for the night. As you can see, Schlemilovitch, being involved in the white slave trade does not preclude being a man of culture. I have spent forty years writing apocrypha, devoting myself to dishonouring the most illustrious writers of France. Take a leaf out of my book, Schlemilovitch! Vengeance, Schlemilovitch, vengeance!'

Later, he introduces me to his henchmen, Mouloud and Mustapha.

'They are at your disposal,' he says, 'I shall send them to you the moment you ask. One never can tell with Aryan women. Sometimes one has to make a show of brute force. Mouloud and Mustapha are peerless when it comes to taming even the most unruly spirits – they're former Waffen SS from the Légion nord-africaine. I met them at Bonny and Laffont's place on Rue Lauriston back when I was secretary to Joanovici. Marvellous fellows. You'll see!'

Mouloud and Mustapha are so alike they could be twins. The same scarred face, the same broken nose, the same disturbing rictus. They immediately show me the greatest kindness.

Lévy-Vendôme accompanies me to the gare Saint-Jean. On the station platform, he hands me three bundles of banknotes.

'For personal expenses. Telephone to keep me up to date. Vengeance, Schlemilovitch! Vengeance! Be ruthless, Schlemilovitch! Vengeance! Ven . . .'

'As you say, *monsieur le vicomte.*'

III

Lake Annecy is romantic, but a young man working in the white slave trade must put such thoughts from his mind.

I catch the first bus for T., a market town I have chosen at random on the Michelin map. The road rises steeply, the hairpin bends make me nauseous. I feel ready to abandon my fine plans. But before long, my taste for the exotic and the desire to air my lungs in the Savoie win out over my despondency. Behind me, a few soldiers start singing 'Les montagnards sont là', and I immediately join in. Then I stroke my wide-rib corduroy trousers, stare down at my clumpy shoes and the alpenstock bought second-hand in a little shop in old Annecy. The tactic I propose to adopt is as follows: in T., I will pass myself off as a young, inexperienced climber who knows of the mountains only from the novels of Frison-Roche. With a little skill, I should quickly ingratiate myself. I can introduce myself to the locals and furtively scout out a young girl worth shipping off to Brazil. For greater security, I have decided to take on the unassailably French identity of my friend Des Essarts. The name Schlemilovitch sounds dubious. The local savages doubtless heard about Jews back when the *Milice* were overrunning the area. The most important thing is not to arouse their suspicions. Suppress my Lévi-Straussian ethnological curiosity. Refrain from staring at their daughter like a horse trader, otherwise they will sniff out my oriental ancestry.

The bus pulls up in front of the church. I sling my rucksack over my shoulder, make my alpenstock ring against the cobbles and stride confidently to the Hôtel des Trois Glaciers. I am immediately captivated by the copper bedstead and the wallpaper in room 13. I telephone Bordeaux to inform Lévy-Vendôme of my arrival and whistle a minuet.

At first, I noticed an unease among the natives. They were unsettled by my tall stature. I knew from experience that one day this would work to my advantage. The first time I crossed the threshold of the Café Municipal, alpenstock in hand, crampons on my shoes, I felt all eyes turn to size me up. Six foot four, five, six, seven? The bets were on. M. Gruffaz, the baker, guessed correctly and scooped the pot and immediately struck up a keen friendship with me. Did M. Gruffaz have a daughter? I would find out soon enough. He introduced me to his friends, the lawyer Forclaz-Manigot and the pharmacist Petit-Savarin. The three men offered me an apple brandy that had me coughing and spluttering. They told me they were waiting for their friend Aravis, a retired colonel, for a game of belote. I asked permission to join them, feeling grateful that Lévy-Vendôme had taught me belote just before I left. I remembered his pertinent remark: 'I should warn you now that working in the white slave trade is not exactly exciting, especially when one is trading in young French girls from the provinces. You must cultivate the interests of a commercial traveller: belote, billiards and aperitifs are the best means of infiltrating these groups.' The three men asked the reason for my stay in T. I explained, as planned, that I was a young French aristocrat with a keen interest in mountaineering.

'Colonel Aravis will like you,' Forclaz-Manigot confided. 'Stout fellow, Aravis, used to be a mountain infantryman. Loves the peaks. Obsessed with climbers. He'll advise you.'

Colonel Aravis arrives and looks me up and down, considering my future as an alpine chasseur. I give him a hearty handshake and click my heels.

'Jean-François Des Essarts! Pleased to meet you, sir!'

'Strapping lad!' he says to the others, 'perfect for the force!'

He becomes paternal:

'I fear, young man, that we don't have time to put you through the rock-climbing exercise that would have given me a better sense of your talents. Never mind, another time. But I guarantee I'll make a seasoned climber out of you. You seem hale and willing and that's the important part!'

My four new friends settle down to playing cards. Outside, it is snowing. I engross myself in reading *L'Écho-Liberté*, the local newspaper. I discover there is a Marx Brothers film playing at the cinema in T. There are six of us, then, six brothers exiled in the Savoie. I feel a little less alone.

On reflection I found the Savoie as charming as I had Guyenne. Was this not the homeland of Henry Bordeaux? When I was about sixteen, I read *Les Roquevillard*, *La Chartreuse du reposoir* and *Le Calvaire du Cimiez* with devotion. A stateless Jew, I hungrily drank in the rustic redolence of these masterpieces. I cannot understand why Henry Bordeaux has fallen from favour in recent years. He had a decisive influence on me and I will be forever loyal to him.

Luckily, I discovered my new-found friends had tastes identical to mine. Aravis read the works of Capitaine Danrit, Petit-Savarin had a weakness for René Bazin and Gruffaz, the baker, set great store by Édouard Estaunié. He had nothing to teach me about the virtues of that particular writer. In *What is literature?*, Des Essarts described the author as follows: 'I consider Édouard Estaunié to be the most deviant author I have ever read. At first glance, Estaunié's characters seem reassuring: paymasters, postmistresses, provincial seminarians, but do not be deceived by appearances: the paymaster has the soul of an anarchist bomber, the postmistress works as a prostitute after her shift at the PTT, the young seminarian is as bloodthirsty as Gilles de Rais . . . Estaunié chose to camouflage vice beneath black frockcoats, mantillas, even soutanes: he is de Sade as petty clerk, he is Genet dragged up as Saint Bernadette of Lourdes.' I read this passage to Forclaz-Manigot, telling him that I had written it. He congratulated me and invited me to dinner. During the meal, I surreptitiously studied his wife. She seemed a little mature, but, if I found nothing better, I decided I would not be choosy. And so, we were living out a novel by Estaunié: the young French aristocrat, so keen on mountaineering, was really a Jew working in the white slave trade; the lawyer's wife, so reserved, so provincial, would all too soon find herself in a Brazilian brothel if I so decided.

Beloved Savoie! To my dying day I will have fond memories of Colonel Aravis. Every little French boy has a grandfather just like him somewhere in the depths of the provinces. He is ashamed of him. Our friend Sartre would like to forget his great-uncle Doctor Schweitzer. When I visit Gide in his ancestral home at Cuverville, he mutters over and over, 'Families, I despise you! Families, I despise you!' Only Aragon, my childhood friend, has not spurned his origins. I am grateful to him for that. When Stalin was alive, he would proudly tell me, 'The Aragons have been cops, father and son, for generations!' One point in his favour. The other two are nothing more than wayward children.

I, Raphäel Schlemilovitch, listened respectfully to my grandfather, Colonel Aravis, as once I had listened to my great-uncle Adrien Debigorre.

'Become a mountain infantryman, Des Essarts, goddammit! You'll be a heart-throb with the ladies. A strapping fellow like you! In uniform, you would turn heads.'

Unfortunately, the uniform of the *chasseurs alpins* reminded me of the *Milice* uniform I had died in twenty years earlier.

'My love of uniforms has never brought me luck,' I explained to the colonel. 'Back in 1894, it got me a notorious trial and several years imprisoned on Devil's Island. The Schlemilovitch Affair, remember?'

The colonel was not listening. He stared me straight in the eye and bellowed:

'Head up, dear boy, please! A strong handshake. Above all don't snigger. We have had enough of seeing the French race denigrated. What we want now is purity.'

I felt very moved. This was just the sort of advice Jo Darnand used to give me when we were battling the Résistance.

Every night, I report back to Lévy-Vendôme. I talk to him about Mme Forclaz-Manigot, the lawyer's wife. He tells me his client in Rio is not interested in mature women. This left me doomed to spending quite some time in the lonely heights of T. I am champing at the bit. Colonel Aravis will be no help, he lives alone. Neither Petit-Savarin nor Gruffaz has daughters. On the other hand, Lévy-Vendôme has specifically forbidden me from meeting young village girls other than through their parents or their husbands: a reputation for being a skirt-chaser would close all doors to me.

IN WHICH THE ABBÉ PERRACHE
GETS ME OUT OF A SCRAPE

I run into this clergyman while in the course of a leisurely stroll around T. Leaning against a tree, he is studying nature, a typical Savoyard parish priest. I am struck by the goodness etched into his face. We strike up a conversation. He talks to me about the Jew Jesus Christ. I talk to him about another Jew named Judas of whom Jesus Christ said 'Good were it for that man if he had never been born!' Our theological discussion continues all the way to the village square. Father Perrache is saddened by my preoccupation with Judas. 'You are a desperate soul,' he tells me gravely, 'despair is the worst sin of all.' I tell this saintly man that my family have sent me to T. to get some fresh air into my lungs and some order into my thoughts. I tell him about my all-too-brief time studying in Bordeaux, explaining that I hated the radical socialist atmosphere of the lycée. He rebukes me for my intransigence. 'Think of Péguy,' he says, 'he divided his time between Chartres cathedral and the *Ligue des insituteurs*. He did his best to teach Jean Jaurès about the glories of Saint Louis and Joan of Arc. One tries not to be too elitist, my son! I tell him I prefer Monsignor Mayol de Lupé: a Catholic should take Christ's interests seriously, even if it means enlisting in the LVF. A Catholic should wield a sword, should declare, like Simon de Montfort, 'God will know His own!' In fact, the Inquisition, in my opinion, was a public health measure. I think it was compassionate of Torquemada and Ximénes to want to cure these people who complacently wallowed in their sickness, in their Jewry; it was kind-hearted of them to offer them a surgical solution rather than leaving them to die of their consumption. After that, I sing the praises of Joseph de Maistre and Édouard Drumont and inform him that God has no time for the mealy-mouthed.

'Neither for the mealy-mouthed nor for the proud,' he tells me, 'and you are committing the sin of Pride, which is just as grave as the sin of Despair. Here, let me set you a little task. You can consider it a penance, an act of contrition. The bishop of this diocese will be visiting the school here in T. a week from now: you will write a welcoming speech which I will pass on to the headmaster. It will be read to His Grace by a young pupil on behalf of the whole community. In it, you will show level-headedness, compassion and humility. Let us pray this exercise brings you back to the path of righteousness! I know you are a lost sheep who wants only to return to the flock. Each man in his darkness goes towards his Light! I have faith in you.' (Sighs.)

A young blonde girl in the garden of the presbytery. She stares at me curiously: Fr. Perrache introduces me to his niece Loïtia. She is wearing the navy blue uniform of a boarding school girl.

Loïtia lights a paraffin lamp. The Savoyard furniture smells of wax polish. I like the chromolithograph on the left-hand wall. The priest gently lays a hand on my shoulder:

'Schlemilovitch, you can write and tell your family that you are now in good hands. I shall see to your spiritual health. The mountain air will do the rest. And now, my boy, you are going to write the welcoming speech for the bishop. Loïtia, could you please bring us tea and some brioches? This man needs to build up his strength.'

I look at Loïtia's pretty face. The nuns at Notre-Dame-des-Fleurs insist that she wear her blonde hair in plaits but, thanks to me, soon she will let it tumble over her shoulders. Having decided to introduce her to the wonders of Brazil, I step into her uncle's study and pen a welcoming speech for His Grace Nuits-Saint-Georges:

'Your Grace,

'In every parish of the noble diocese that it has pleased Providence to entrust to him, the Bishop Nuits-Saint-Georges is welcome, bringing as he does the comfort of his presence and the precious blessings of his ministry.

'But he is particularly welcome here in the picturesque valley of T., renowned for its many-hued mantle of meadows and forests . . .

'This same valley which a historian of recent memory called "a land of priests fondly attached to their spiritual leaders". Here in this school built through magnanimous, sometimes heroic gestures . . . Your Grace is at home here . . . and an eddy of joyous impetuousness, stirring our little universe, has anticipated and solemnised your arrival.

'Your Grace, you bring the comfort of your support and the light of your counsel to the teachers, your devoted collaborators whose task is a particularly thankless one; you bestow upon the pupils, the benevolence of your fatherly smile and an interest of which they strive to be deserving . . . We joyfully commend you as an informed educator, a friend to youth, a zealous promoter of all things that foster the influence of Christian Schools – a living reality and the promise of a bright future of our country.

'For you, Your Grace, the well-tended lawns that flank the gates are freshly coiffed and a scattering of flowers – despite the bleakness of the season – sing their symphony of colours; for you, our House, ordinarily a buzzing, boisterous hive, is filled with contemplation and with silence; for you, the somewhat humdrum rhythm of classes and courses has interrupted its flow . . . This is a great and holy day, a day of serene joy and of good resolutions!

'We wish to participate, Your Grace, in the great work of renewal and reconstruction on the building sites excavated in this new era by the Church and by France. Honoured by your visit and mindful of such counsel as you choose to offer, with joyful hearts we offer Your Grace the traditional filial salute:

'Blessed be Bishop Nuits-Saint-Georges,

'*Heil* to His Grace our Bishop!'

I hope my work pleases Father Perrache and allows me to cultivate our precious friendship: my career in the white slave trade depends on it.

Fortunately, he dissolves into tears as he reads from the first lines and lavishes me with praise. He will personally share the delights of my prose with the headmaster.

Loïtia is sitting by the fire. Her head is tilted to one side, she has the pensive look of a girl in a Botticelli painting. She will be a big hit in the brothels of Rio next summer.

Canon Saint-Gervais, the school principal, was very satisfied with my speech. At our first meeting, he suggested I might replace the history teacher, Fr. Ivan Canigou, who had disappeared without leaving a forwarding address. According to Saint-Gervais, Fr. Canigou, a handsome man, had been unable to resist his vocation as a missionary and planned to convert the Gentiles of Xinjiang; he would not be seen again in T. Through Fr. Perrache, the Canon knew of my studies for the *École Normale Supèrieure* and had no doubts as to my talents as a historian.

'You would take over from Fr. Canigou until we can find a new history teacher. It will give you something to keep you occupied. What do you say?'

I raced to break the good news to Fr. Perrache.

'I personally implored the Canon to find something to occupy your free time. Idleness is not good for you. To work, my child! You are back on the right path! Take care not to stray again!'

I asked his permission to play belote which he readily gave. At the Café Municipal, Colonel Aravis, Forclaz-Manigot and Petit-Savarin greeted me warmly. I told them of my new post and we drank plum brandy from the Meuse and clapped each other on the back.

At this particular point in my biography, I think it best to consult the newspapers. Did I enter a seminary as Perrache advised me? Henry Bordeaux's article 'Fr. Raphäel Schlemilovitch: a new "Curé d'Ars"' (*Action française*, October 23, 19—) would seem to suggest as much: the novelist compliments me for the apostolic zeal I show in the tiny Savoie village of T.

Meanwhile, I take long walks in the company of Loïtia. Her delightful uniform and her hair colour my Saturdays navy blue and blonde. We bump into Colonel Aravis, who gives us a knowing smile. Forclaz-Manigot and Petit-Savarin have even offered to stand witness at our wedding. Gradually, I forget the reasons why I came to Savoie and the sardonic smirk of Lévy-Vendôme. No, I will never deliver the innocent Loïtia into the hands of Brazilian pimps. I will settle permanently in T. Peacefully and humbly, I will go to work as a schoolteacher. By my side, I shall have a loving wife, an old priest, a kindly colonel, a genial lawyer and a pharmacist . . . Rain claws at the windows, the fire in the hearth gives off a gentle glow, *monsieur l'abbé* is speaking to me softly, Loïtia is bent over her needlework. From time to time our eyes meet. Fr. Perrache asks me to recite a poem . . .

My heart, smile towards the future now . . .
The bitter words I have allayed
And darkling dreams have sent away.

And then:

. . . The fireside, the lamplight's slender beam . . .

At night, in my cramped hotel room, I write the first part of my memoir to be rid of my turbulent youth. I gaze confidently at the mountains and the forests, the Café Municipal and the church. The Jewish contortions are over. I hate the lies that caused me so much pain. The earth, the earth does not lie.

Chest proudly puffed with fine resolutions, I took wing and set off to teach the history of France. Before my pupils, I indulged in a wild courtship of Joan of Arc. I set off on all the Crusades, I fought at Bouvines, at Rocroi, on the bridge at Arcola. I quickly realised, alas, that I lacked the *furia francese*. The blonde chevaliers outpaced me as we marched and the banners with their fleurs-de-lis fell from my hands. A Yiddish woman's lament spoke to me of a death that wore no spurs, no plumes, no white gloves.

In the end, when I could bear it no longer, I pointed my forefinger at Cran-Gevrier, my best pupil:

'It was a Jew who broke the vase of Soissons! A Jew, d'you hear me! Write out a hundred times "It was a Jew who broke the vase of Soissons!" Learn your lessons, Cran-Gevrier! No marks, Cran-Gevrier! You will stay back after class!'

Cran-Gevrier started to sob. So did I.

I stalked out of the classroom and sent a telegram to Lévy-Vendôme to tell him I would deliver Loïtia the following Saturday. I suggested Geneva as a possible rendezvous for the handover. Then, I stayed up until three o'clock in the morning writing a critique of myself, 'A Jew in the Countryside', in which I derided my weakness for the French provinces. I did not mince words: 'Having been a collaborationist Jew like Joanovici-Sachs, Raphäel Schlemilovitch is now playing out a "Back to the land" shtick of a Barrès-Pétain. How long before we get the squalid farce of the militarist Jew like Capitaine Dreyfus-Stroheim? The self-loathing Jew like Simone Weil-Céline? The eminent Jew in the mould of Proust-Daniel Halévy-Maurois? We would like Raphäel Schlemilovitch simply to be a Jew . . .'

This act of contrition done, the world once again took on the colours that I love. Spotlights raked the village square, boots pounded the cobbled streets. Colonel Aravis was rudely awakened, as were Forclaz-Manigot, Gruffaz,

Petit-Savarin, Fr. Perrache, my best pupil Cran-Gevrier and my fiancée Loïtia. They were interrogated about me. A Jew hiding out in the Haute-Savoie. A dangerous Jew. Public enemy number one. There was a price on my head. When had they last seen me? My friends would unquestionably turn me in. The *Milice* were already on their way to the Hôtel des Trois Glaciers. They broke down the door to my room. And there, sprawled on my bed, I waited, yes, I waited and whistled a minuet.

I drink my last plum brandy at the Café Municipal. Colonel Aravis, the lawyer Forclaz-Manigot, the pharmacist Petit-Savarin and Gruffaz the baker wish me a safe journey.

'I'll be back tomorrow night for our game of belote,' I promise, 'I'll bring you some Swiss chocolate.'

I tell Fr. Perrache that my father is staying in a hotel in Geneva and would like to spend the evening with me. He makes a little something for me to eat and tells me not to dawdle on the way back.

I get off the bus at Veyrier-du-Lac and take up my position outside Notre-Dame-des-Fleurs. Soon afterwards, Loïtia comes through the wrought iron gates. After that, everything goes as I had planned. Her eyes shine as I talk to her of love, of empty promises, of abductions, of adventures, of swashbucklers. I lead her to Annecy coach station. From there we take a bus to Geneva. Cruseilles, Annemasse,

Saint-Julien, Geneva, Rio de Janeiro. Giraudoux's girls love to travel. This one, however, seems a little anxious. She reminds me she doesn't have a suitcase. Don't worry. We'll buy everything we need when we get there. I'll introduce her to my father, Vicomte Lévy-Vendôme, who will shower her with gifts. He's very sweet, you'll see. Bald. He has a monocle and a long jade cigarette-holder. Don't be scared. This gentleman means well. We cross the border. Quickly. We drink fruit juice at the bar of the Hôtel des Bergues while we wait for the vicomte. He strides up to us, flanked by his henchmen Mouloud and Mustapha. Quickly. He puffs nervously on his jade cigarette-holder. He adjusts his monocle and hands me an envelope stuffed with dollars.

'Your wages! I'll take care of the young lady! You have no time to lose! From Savoie you go to Normandy! Call me on my Bordeaux number as soon as you arrive!'

Loïtia gives me a panicked glance. I tell her I will be right back.

That night, I walked along the banks of the Rhône thinking of Jean Giraudoux, of Colette, Marivaux, Verlaine, Charles d'Orléans, Maurice Scève, Rémy Belleau and Corneille. I am coarse and crude compared to such people. I am unworthy. I ask their forgiveness for being born in the Île-de-France rather than Vilnius, Lithuania. I scarcely dare write in French: such a delicate language putrefies beneath my pen . . .

I scrawl another fifty pages. After that, I shall give up literature. I swear it.

In Normandy, I will put the finishing touches to my sentimental education. Fougeire-Jusquiames, a little town in Calvados, set off by a seventeenth-century château. As in T., I take a hotel room. This time, I pass myself off as a sales representative for exotic foods. I offer the manageress of Les Trois-Vikings some Turkish delight and question her about the lady of the manor, Véronique de Fougeire-Jusquiames. She tells me everything she knows: *madame la marquise* lives alone, the villagers see her only at high mass on Sundays. Every year, she organises a hunt. Tourists are allowed to visit the château on Saturday afternoons for three hundred francs a head. Gérard, the Marquise's chauffeur, acts as guide.

That same evening, I telephone Lévy-Vendôme to tell him I have arrived in Normandy. He implores me to carry out my mission as quickly as possible: our client, the Emir of Samandal, has been daily sending impatient telegrams threatening to cancel the contract if the merchandise is not delivered within the week. Clearly, Lévy-Vendôme does not understand the difficulties I face. How can I, Raphäel Schlemilovitch, make the acquaintance of a marquise overnight? Especially since I am not in Paris, but in Fougeire-Jusquiames, in the heart of rural France. Around here, no Jew, however handsome, would be allowed anywhere near the château except on Saturdays with all the other paying guests.

I spend all night studying a dossier compiled by Lévy-Vendôme on the lineage of the marquise. Her pedigree is excellent. The *Directory of French Nobility*, founded in 1843 by Baron Samuel Bloch-Morel, offers the following summary: 'FOUGEIRE-JUSQUIAMES: Seat: Normandie-Poitou. Lineage: Jourdain de Jusquiames, a natural son of Eleanor of Aquitaine. Motto: "Jusquiames, do or damn, Fougère ne'er despair." The House of Jusquiames supplants the earlier comtes de Fougeire in 1385. Title: duc de Jusquiames (hereditary duchy) under letters patent of 20 September 1603; made hereditary member of the *Chambre des pairs* by the decree of 30 August 1817. Hereditary Duke-Peer (duc de Jusquiame) Cadet branch: *baron romain*, papal brief of 19 June 1819, ratified by the decree of 7 September 1822; prince with right of transmission to all descendants by decree of the King of Bavaria of 6 March 1846. Advanced to the dignity of hereditary Count-Peer, by the edict of June 10, 1817. Arms: Gules on a field Azure, Fleurs-De-Lis sautéed with Stars per Saltire.'

In their chronicles of the Fourth Crusade, Robert de Clary, Villehardouin and Henri de Valenciennes offer testaments to the good conduct of the Seigneurs de Fougeire, Froissard, Commynes and Montluc and heap praise upon the valiant Capitaine de Jusquiames. In chapter X of his history of Saint Louis, Joinville recalls a good deed by a knight of the de Fougeire family: 'Then did this right worthy man raise up his sword and smite the Jew 'twixt the eyes dashing him to the ground. And lo! the Jews did turn and flee taking with them their wounded master.'

On Sunday morning, he posted himself at the entrance to the church. Shortly before eleven o'clock, a black limousine pulled into the square; his heart was pounding. A blonde woman was walking towards him but he dared not look at her. He followed her into the church, struggling to master his emotions. How pure her profile was! Above her, a stained glass window depicted the entrance of Eleanor of Aquitaine into Jerusalem. She looked just like the Marquise de Fougeire-Jusquiames. The same blonde hair, the same tilt of the head, the same slender, delicate neck. His eyes moved from marquise to queen and he thought: 'How beautiful she is! What nobleness! I see before me a proud Jusquiames, a descendant of Eleanor of Aquitaine.' Or 'The glories of the Jusquiames precede the reign of Charlemagne, they held the power of life and death over their vassals. The Marquise de Jusquiames is descended in direct line from Eleanor of Aquitaine. She neither knows nor would she deign to know any of the people gathered here.' Certainly not Schlemilovitch. He decided to abandon his efforts: Lévy-Vendôme would surely understand that they had been presumptuous. To transform Eleanor of Aquitaine into the denizen of a brothel. The prospect was repugnant.

One may be called Schlemilovitch and yet nurture a flicker of sensitivity in one's heart. The organ and the hymns awakened his nobler disposition. Never would he give up this princess, this fairy, this saint of the Saracens. He would strive to be her hireling, a Jewish pageboy, granted, but mores have changed since the twelfth century and the Marquise de Fougeire-Jusquiames would not take offence at his origins. He would take on the identity of his friend Des Essarts so he might more readily introduce himself. He would talk to her about his own forebears, about Foulques Des Essarts who gutted two hundred Jews before setting off for the Crusades. Foulques was right to do so, these Jews boiled the Host, their slaughter was too kind a punishment, for the bodies of even a thousand Jews are not the equivalent of the sacred Body of Our Lord.

As she left the mass, the Marquise glanced distantly at her congregation. Was it some illusion? Her eyes of periwinkle blue seemed to fix on him. Did she sense the devotion he had vowed to her not an hour since?

He raced across the church square. When the black limousine was only twenty metres away, he collapsed in the middle of the road, pretending a fainting fit. He heard the brakes squeal. A mellifluous voice murmured:

'Gérard, help that poor young man into the car! A sudden malaise no doubt! His face is so pale! We will prepare a hot toddy for him at the château.'

He was careful not to open his eyes. The back seat on which the chauffeur laid him smelled of Russian leather but he had only to repeat to himself the sweet name of Jusquiames for a scent of violets and brushwood to caress his nose. He was dreaming of the blonde tresses of Princess Eleanor, of the château towards which he was gliding. Not for a moment did it occur to him that, having been a collaborationist Jew, a bookish Jew, a bucolic Jewish, he was now in danger, in this limousine emblazoned with the Marquise's coat of arms (Gules on a field Azure, Fleurs-De-Lis sautéed with Stars per Saltire), of becoming a snobbish Jew.

The Marquise asked him no questions as though she found his presence entirely natural. They strolled together through the grounds of the château, she showed him the flowers and the beautiful spring waters. Then, they went up to the house. He admired the portrait of Cardinal de Fougeire-Jusquiames. He found the Marquise enchanting. The inflections of her voice were pierced by the jagged contours of the land itself. Subjugated, he murmured to himself: 'The energy and charm of a cruel little girl of one of the noble families of France who from her childhood had been brought up in the saddle, had tortured cats, gouged out the eyes of rabbits . . .'

After a candlelit dinner served by Gérard, they sat and chatted by the monumental fireplace in the drawing room.

The Marquise talked to him about herself, about her grandparents, her uncles and cousins . . . Soon, nothing of the Fougeire-Jusquiames family was unknown to him.

I stroke a Claude Lorrain hanging on the left-hand wall of my bedroom: *The Embarkation of Eleanor of Aquitaine for the Orient*. Then I study Watteau's *Sad Harlequin*. I step around the Savonnerie carpet, fearful of soiling it. I do not deserve such a prestigious room. Nor the *epée de page* – the little sword upon the mantel. Nor the Philippe de Champaigne that hangs next to my bed, a bed in which Louis XIV slept with Mlle de La Vallière. From my window, I see a woman on horseback galloping through the grounds. For the Marquise goes every morning at five o'clock to ride Bayard, her favourite horse. At a fork in the path, she disappears. Nothing now disturbs the silence. And so I decide to embark upon a sort of biographical novel. I have memorised every detail the Marquise graciously gave me on the subject of her family. I shall use them to write the first volume of the work, which will be called *The Fougeire-Jusquiames Way, or the Memoirs of Saint-Simon as revised by Scheherazade and a handful of Talmudic Scholars*. In my childhood days, on the quai Conti in Paris, Miss Evelyn would read me the *Thousand and One Nights* and the *Memoirs* of Saint-Simon. Then she would turn out the light. She would leave the door to my room ajar so that I might hear, before I fell asleep, Mozart's

Serenade in G major. Taking advantage of my drowsy state, Scheherazade and the Duc de Saint-Simon would cast shadows with a magic lantern. I would see the Princesse des Ursins step into the caves of Ali Baba, watch the marriage of Aladdin and Mlle de la Vallière, the abduction of Mme Soubise by the caliph Harun al-Rashid. The splendours of the Orient mingling with those of Versailles created a magical world which I will try to recreate in my novel.

Night falls, the Marquise de Fougeire-Jusquiames passes beneath my window on horseback. She is the faerie Mélusine, she is *La Belle aux cheveux d'or.* Nothing has changed since those days when my English governess read to me. Miss Evelyn would often take me to the Louvre. We had only to cross the Seine. Claude Lorrain, Philippe de Champaigne, Watteau, Delacroix, Corot coloured my childhood. Mozart and Haydn lulled it. Scheherazade and Saint-Simon brightened it. An exceptional childhood, a magical childhood I should tell you about. Immediately, I begin *The Fougeire-Jusquiames Way.* On a sheet of vellum bearing the arms of the Marquise, in a nervous hand, I write: 'It was, this "Fougeire-Jusquiames", like the setting of a novel, an imaginary landscape which I could with difficulty picture to myself and longed all the more to discover, set in the midst of real lands and roads which all of a sudden would become alive with heraldic details . . .'

This evening, they did not converse in front of the hearth as usual. The Marquise ushered him into a large boudoir papered in blue and adjoining her chamber. A candelabra cast a flickering glow. The floor was strewn with crimson cushions. On the walls hung bawdy prints by Moreau le Jeune, Girard and Binet, a painting in an austere style that might have been the work of Hyacinthe Rigaud depicted Eleanor of Aquitaine about to give herself to Saladin, the leader of the Saracens.

The door opened. The Marquise was dressed in a gauze dress that left her breasts free.

'Your name is Schlemilovitch, isn't it?' she asked in a coarse accent he had never heard her use. 'Born in Boulogne-Billancourt? I read it on your identity card! A Jew? I love it! My great-great-uncle Palamède de Jusquiames said nasty things about Jews but he admired Marcel Proust! The Fougeire-Jusquiames, or at least the women in the family, are not prejudiced against Orientals. My ancestor, Eleanor, took advantage of the Second Crusade to cavort with Saracens while the miserable Louis VII was sacking Damascus! In 1720, another of my ancestors, the Marquise de Jusquiames, found the Turkish ambassador's son very much to her taste! On that subject, I notice you have compiled a whole Fougeire-Jusquiames dossier! I am flattered by the interest you take in our family! I even read the charming little passage, no doubt inspired by your stay at the château: 'It was, this "Fougeire-Jusquiames", like the setting of a novel,

an imaginary landscape . . .' Do you take yourself for Marcel
Proust, Schlemilovitch? That seems ominous! Surely you're
not going to waste your youth copying out *In Search of Lost
Time*? I warn you now, I'm not some fairy from your childhood! Sleeping Beauty! The Duchesse de Guermantes! *La
femme-fleur*. You're wasting your time! Treat me like some
whore from the Rue des Lombards, stop drooling over my
aristocratic titles! My field Azure with fleurs-de-lis.
Villehardouin, Froissart, Saint-Simon and all that lot!
Snobbish little Jewish socialite! Enough of the quavering, the
bowing and scraping! I find those gigolo good looks of yours
devilishly arousing! Electrifying! Handsome thug! Charming
pimp! Pretty boy! Catamite! Do you really think Fougeire-
Jusquiames is "like the setting of a novel, an imaginary
landscape"? It's a brothel, don't you see? The château has
always been a high-class brothel. Very popular during the
German occupation. My late father, Charles de Fougeire-
Jusquiames, pimped for French intellectual collaborators.
Statues by Arno Breker, young Luftwaffe pilots, SS Officers,
Hitlerjugend, everything was arranged for the pleasure of
these gentlemen! My father understood that sex often deter-
mines one's political fortunes. Now, let's talk about you,
Schlemilovitch! Let's not waste time! You're a Jew? I suppose
you'd like to rape a queen of France. I have various costumes
up in the attic. Would you like me to dress as Anne of Austria,
my angel? Blanche de Navarre? Marie Leszczyńska? Or
would you rather fuck Adélaïde de Savoie? Marguerite de

Provence? Jeanne d'Albret? Choose! I'll dress up a thousand different ways. Tonight, all the queens of France will be your whores . . .'

The week that ensued was truly idyllic: the Marquise constantly changed her costume to rekindle his desires. Together with the queens of France, he ravished Mme de Chevreuse, the Duchesse de Berry, the Chevalier d'Éon, Bossuet, Saint Louis, Bayard, Du Guesclin, Joan of Arc, the Comte de Toulouse and Général Boulanger.

He spent the rest of his time getting better acquainted with Gérard.

'My chauffeur enjoys an excellent reputation in the underworld,' confided Véronique. 'The gangsters call him The Undertaker or Gérard the Gestapo. Gérard was one of the Rue Lauriston gang. He was my late father's secretary, his henchman . . .'

His own father had also encountered Gérard the Gestapo. He had mentioned him during their time in Bordeaux. On 16 July 1942 Gérard had bundled Schlemilovitch *père* into a black truck: 'What do you say to an identity check at the Rue Lauriston and a little spell in Drancy?' Schlemilovitch *fils* no longer remembered by what miracle Schlemilovitch *père* escaped the clutches of this good man.

One night, leaving the Marquise, you surprised Gérard leaning on the balustrade of the veranda.

'You like the moonlight? The still pale moonlight, sad and fair? A romantic, Gérard?'

He did not have time to answer you. You grabbed his throat. The cervical vertebrae cracked slightly. You have a distasteful penchant for desecrating corpses. With the blade of a Gillette Extra-Blue, you slice away the ears. Then the eyelids. Then you gouge the eyes from their sockets. All that remained was to smash the teeth. Three heel kicks were enough.

Before burying Gérard, you considered having him stuffed and sent to your poor father, but you could no longer remember the address of Schlemilovitch Ltd., New York.

All loves are short-lived. The Marquise, dressed as Eleanor of Aquitaine, will succumb, but the sound of a car will interrupt our frolics. The brakes will shriek. I will be surprised to hear a gypsy melody. The drawing room door will be suddenly flung open. A man in a red turban will appear. Despite his fakir outfit, I will recognise the vicomte Charles Lévy-Vendôme.

Three fiddle players will appear behind him and launch into a second *czardas*. Mouloud and Mustapha will bring up the rear.

'What is going on, Schlemilovitch?' the vicomte will ask. 'We have had no news from you in days!'

He will wave to Mouloud and Mustapha.

'Take this woman to the Buick and keep a close eye on her. My apologies, madame, for bursting in unannounced, but we have no time to lose! You see, you were expected in Beirut a week ago!'

A few power slaps from Mouloud will snuff out any vague inclination to resist. Mustapha will gag and bind my companion.

'It's in the bag!' Lévy-Vendôme will quip as his henchmen drag Véronique away.

The vicomte will adjust his monocle.

'Your mission has been a fiasco. I expected you to deliver the Marquise to Paris, instead of which I was personally forced to come to Fougeire-Jusquiames. You are fired, Schlemilovitch! Now, let us talk of something else. Enough melodrama for one evening. I propose we take a tour of this magnificent house in the company of our musicians. We are the new lords of Fougeire-Jusquiames. The Marquise is about to bequeath us all her worldly goods. Whether she wishes to or not!'

I can still picture that curious character with his turban and his monocle exploring the château, candelabra in hand, while the violinists played gypsy airs. He spent some time studying the portrait of cardinal de Fougeire-Jusquiames, stroked a suit of armour that had belonged to an ancestor, Jourdain, a natural son of Eleanor of Aquitaine. I showed him my bedrooms, the Watteau, the Claude Lorrain, the Philippe de Champaigne and the bed in which Louis XIV and Mlle de La Vallière had slept. He read the short passage I had written on the emblazoned paper: 'It was, this "Fougeire-Jusquiames" . . .' etc. He gave me a spiteful look. At that moment, the musicians were playing *Wiezenlied*, a Yiddish lullaby.

'Decidedly, Schlemilovitch, your time here at Fougeire-Jusquiames did not do you much good! The scents of old France have quite turned your head. When is the christening? Planning to be a 100 per cent pureblood Frenchman? I have to put a stop to your ridiculous daydreams. Read the Talmud instead of poring over histories of the Crusades. Stop slavering over the heraldic almanacs . . . Take my word for it, the star of David is worth more than all these "chevrons à sinoples" or "Gules, two lion passants", or "Azure, three fleurs-de-lis d'or". You don't imagine you're Charles Swann, do you? You're not planning to apply for membership of the Jockey Club? To join the social whirl of the Faubourg Saint-Germain? You may remember that Charles Swann himself, that idol of duchesses, arbiter of elegance, darling of the Guermantes, remembered his origins when he grew old. If I might be permitted, Schlemilovitch?'

The vicomte gestured to the violinists to interrupt their playing and, in a stentorian voice, declaimed:

'Perhaps too, in these last days, the physical type that characterises his race was becoming more pronounced in him, at the same time as a sense of moral solidarity with the rest of the Jews, a solidarity which Swann seemed to have forgotten throughout his life, and which, one after another, his mortal illness, the Dreyfus case and the anti-Semitic propaganda had revived . . .'

'We always return to our own people, Schlemilovitch! Even after long years of straying!'

In a monotone he recited:

'The Jew is the substance of God; non-Jews are but cattle seed; non-Jews are created to serve Jews. We order that every Jew, three times each day, should curse the Christian peoples and call upon God to exterminate them with their kings and princes. The Jew who rapes or despoils a non-Jewish woman or even kills her must be absolved in justice for he has wronged only a mare.'

He removed his turban and put on a false, preposterously hooked nose.

'You've never seen me play the role of Süss the Jew? Picture it, Schlemilovitch! I have just killed the Marquise, I have drunk her blood like a self-respecting vampire. The blood of Eleanor of Aquitaine and her valiant knights! Now I unfold my vulture's wings. I grimace. I contort myself. Musicians, please, play your wildest *czardas*. See my hands, Schlemilovitch! The nails like talons! Louder, musicians, louder! I cast a venomous glance at the Watteau, the Philippe de Champaigne, I will rip up the Savonnerie carpet with my claws! Slash the old master paintings! In a short while, I will run about the château howling in a terrifying manner. I will overturn the crusaders' suits of armour! When I have sated my rage, I will sell this ancestral home. Preferably to a South American magnate. The king of *guano*, for example. With the money I shall buy sixty pairs of crocodile-skin moccasins, emerald green alpaca suits, panther-skin coats, ribbed shirts with orange stripes. I shall have thirty mistresses, Yemenites, Ethiopians, Circassians. What do you think, Schlemilovitch? Don't be afraid, my boy, all this hides a deep sentimental streak.'

There was a moment of silence. Lévy-Vendôme gestured for me to follow him. Outside on the steps of the château, he whispered.

'Let me be alone, please. Leave immediately. Travel forms the young mind. Go east, Schlemilovitch, go east! A pilgrimage to the source: Vienna, Constantinople, the banks of the Jordan. I am almost tempted to go with you. Leave France as soon as possible! Go! This country has wronged you. You have taken root here. Never forget that we are the international association of fakirs and prophets. Have no fear, you will see me again. I am needed in Constantinople to engineer the gradual halt to the cycle. Gradually the seasons will change, first the spring, then the summer. Astronomers and meteorologists know nothing, take my word for this, Schlemilovitch. I shall disappear from Europe towards the end of the century and go to the Himalayas. I will rest. I will reappear here eighty-five years to the day from now, sporting the sidelocks and beard of a rabbi. Goodbye for now. I love you.'

IV

Vienna. The last tramways glided into the night. On Mariahilfer Straße, we felt fear overcoming us. A few more steps and we would find ourselves on the Place de la Concorde. Take the métro, count off the reassuring rosary: Tuileries, Palais-Royal, Louvre, Châtelet. Our mother would be waiting for us, Quai Conti. We would drink lime-blossom and mint *tisane* and watch the shadows cast on the walls of our bedroom by the passing river boats. Never had we loved Paris more, nor France. A winter's night, a Jewish painter, our cousin, staggering around Montparnasse, muttering as he died *'Cara, cara Italia'*. By chance he had been born in Livorno, he might have been born in Paris, in London, in Warsaw, anywhere. We were born in Boulogne-sur-Seine, Île-de-France. Far from here, Tuileries. Palais-Royal, Châtelet. The exquisite Mme de La Fayette. Choderlos de Laclos. Benjamin Constant, dear old Stendhal. Fate had played us a cruel trick. We would not see our country again. Die on Mariahilfer Straße like stray dogs. No one could protect us. Our mother was dead or mad. We did not know our father's New York address. Nor that of Maurice Sachs. Or Adrien Debigorre. As for Charles Lévy-Vendôme, there was no point calling on him. Tania Arcisewska was dead because she had taken our advice. Des Essarts was dead. Loïtia was probably slowly becoming accustomed to far-flung brothels. We made no effort to clasp them to us, these faces that passed through our lives, to cling to them, to love them. Incapable of the slightest act.

We arrived at the Burggarten and sat on one of the benches. Suddenly we heard the sound of a wooden leg striking the ground. A man was walking towards us, a monstrous cripple . . . His eyes were luminous, his sweeping fringe and his stubby moustache glistened in the darkness. His lips were set in a rictus that made our hearts pound. His left arm, which he extended, tapered to a hook. We had expected to run into him in Vienna. Inevitably. He was wearing the uniform of an Austrian corporal the better to terrify us. He threatened us, bellowing: '*Sechs Millionen Juden! Sechs Millionen Juden!*' Shrapnel from his booming laugh pierced our chests. He tried to gouge our eyes out with his hook. We ran away. He followed us, shrieking: '*Sechs Millionen Juden! Sechs Millionen Juden!*' For a long time we ran through the dead city, this drowned city washed up on the shore. Hofburg, Palais Kinsky, Palais Lobkowitz, Palais Pallavicini, Palais Porcia, Palais Wilczek . . . Behind us, in a rasping voice Captain Hook sang 'Hitlerleute', thumping the pavement with his wooden leg. It seemed to us we were the only people in the city. After killing us, our enemy would wander these empty streets like a ghost until the end of time.

The streetlights along the Graben help me see things more clearly. Three American tourists persuade me that

Hitler is long since dead. I follow them, trailing a few metres behind. They turn onto Dorotheergasse and go into the nearest café. I take a table at the back. I don't have a *schilling* and I tell the waiter I am waiting for someone. With a smile, he brings me a newspaper. I discover that last night, at midnight, Albert Speer and Baldur von Schirach left Spandau prison in a big black Mercedes. At a press conference in the Hilton Hotel in Berlin, Schirach declared: 'Sorry to have kept you waiting so long.' In the photo, he is wearing a turtleneck sweater. Cashmere, probably. *Made in Scotland*. Gentleman. Former Gauleiter of Vienna. Fifty thousand Jews.

A young, dark-haired woman, chin resting on her open palm. I wonder what she is doing here, alone, so forlorn among the beer drinkers. Surely she belongs to that race of humans I have chosen above all other: their features are harsh and yet delicate, in their faces you can see their enduring loyalty to grief. Anyone but Raphäel Schlemilovitch would take these anaemics by the hand and beg them to make their peace with life. As for me, those I love, I kill. And so I choose those who are weak, defenceless. To take an example, I killed my mother with grief. She demonstrated exceptional meekness. She would beg me to have my tuberculosis treated. I would gruffly snap: 'You don't treat tuberculosis, you nurture it, you cherish it like a dancehall girl.' My mother would hang her head.

Later, Tania asks me to protect her. I hand her a razor blade, a Gillette Extra-Blue. In the end, I anticipated her wishes: she would have been bored living with a fat man. Slyly suicided while he was singing the praises of nature in springtime. As for Des Essarts, my brother, my only friend, was it not I who tampered with the brakes of the car so he could safely shatter his skull?

The young woman looks at me with astonished eyes. I remember something Lévy-Vendôme said: force an entry into other people's lives. I take a seat at her table. She gives a faint smile of a melancholy I find ravishing. I immediately decide to trust her. And besides, she is dark. Blond hair, pink complexions, porcelain eyes get on my nerves. Everything that radiates health and happiness turns my stomach. Racist after my fashion. Such prejudices are forgivable in a young consumptive Jew.

'Are you coming?' she says.

There is such gentleness in her voice that I resolve to write a beautiful novel and dedicate it to her: '*Schlemilovitch in the Land of Women*'. In it, I will show how a little Jew seeks refuge among women in moments of distress. Without women, the world would be unbearable. Men are too serious. Too absorbed in their elegant abstractions, their vocations: politics, art, the textile business. They have to respect you before they will help you. Incapable of an unselfish action. Sensible. Dismal. Miserly. Pretentious. Men would leave me to starve to death.

We leave the Dorotheergasse. After this point, my memories are hazy. We walk back along the Graben and turn left. We go into a café much larger than the first. I drink, I eat, I recover my health while Hilda – that is her name – gazes at me fondly. Around us, every table is occupied by several women. Whores. Hilda is a whore. In the person of Raphäel Schlemilovitch, she has just found her pimp. In future, I will call her Marizibill: when Apollinaire wrote about the 'Jewish pimp, red-haired and ruddy-faced' he was thinking of me. I own this place: the waiter who brings me my *alcools* looks like Lévy-Vendôme. German soldiers come to my establishment to console themselves before setting off for the Eastern Front. Heydrich himself sometimes visits. He has a soft spot for Tania, Loïtia and Hilda, my prettiest whores. He feels no revulsion when he straddles Tania, the Jewess. Besides, Heydrich himself is a *Mischling*. Given his lieutenant's zeal, Hitler turned a blind eye. I have similarly been spared, Raphäel Schlemilovitch, the biggest pimp of the Third Reich. My girls have been my shield. Thanks to them I will not know Auschwitz. If, by chance, the Gauleiter of Vienna should change his mind about me, in a day Tania, Loïtia and Hilda could collect the money for my ransom. I imagine five hundred thousand Reichsmarks would suffice, given that a Jew is not worth the rope required to hang him. The Gestapo will look the other way and let me disappear to South America. No point dwelling on such things: thanks to Tania, Loïtia and Hilda I have considerable influence over Heydrich. From him, they can get a document countersigned by Himmler certifying that I am an honorary citizen of the Third Reich. The Indispensable Jew. When you have women to protect you, everything falls into place. Since 1935, I have been the lover of Eva Braun. Chancellor Hitler was always leaving her alone at the Berchtesgaden. I immediately begin to think how I might turn this situation to my advantage.

I am skulking around the Berghof when I meet Eva for the first time. The instant attraction is mutual. Hitler comes to Obersalzberg once a month. We get along very well. He gracefully accepts my role as escort to Eva. Such things seem to him so futile . . . In the evenings, he tells us about his plans. We listen, like two children. He has given me the honorary title of SS Brigadenführer. I should dig out the photo on which Eva wrote *'Für mein kleiner Jude, mein gelibter Schlemilovitch – Seine Eva.'*

Hilda gently lays a hand on my shoulder. It is late, the customers have left the café. The waiter is reading *Der Stern* by the bar. Hilda gets up and slips a coin into the jukebox. Instantly, the voice of Zarah Leander lulls me like a gentle, husky river. She sings 'Ich stehe im Regen' – 'I am standing in the rain'. She sings 'Mit roten Rosen fängt die Liebe meistens an' – 'Love always begins with red roses'. It often ends with Gillette Extra-Blue razor blades.

The waiter asks us to leave the café. We walk along a desolate avenue. Where am I? Vienna? Geneva? Paris? And this woman clutching my arm, is she Tania, Loïtia, Hilda, Eva Braun? Later, we find ourselves standing in the middle of an esplanade in front of an illuminated basilica. The Sacré-Cœur? I slump onto the seat of a hydraulic lift. A door is opened. A vast white-walled bedroom. A four-poster bed. I fall asleep.

The following day, I got to know Hilda, my new friend. Despite her dark hair and her delicate face, she was a little Aryan girl, half-German, half-Austrian. From her wallet, she took several photographs of her father and her mother. Both dead. The former in Berlin during the bombings, the latter disembowelled by Cossacks. I was sorry I had never known Herr Murzzuschlag, a stiff SS officer and perhaps my future father-in-law. I was much taken by their wedding photograph: Murzzuschlag and his young bride in Bruxelles, intriguing passers-by with his immaculate uniform and the contemptuous jut of his chin. This was not just anybody: a friend of Rudolph Hess and Goebbels, on first name terms with Himmler. Hitler himself, when awarding him the Cross of Merit, said 'Skorzeny and Murzzuschlag never let me down.'

Why had I not met Hilda in the thirties? Frau Murzzuschlag makes *kneidel* for me, her husband fondly pats my cheeks and says:

'You're a Jew? We'll sort that out, my boy! Marry my daughter! I'll take care of the rest! *Der treue Heinrich** will understand.'

I thank him, but I do not need his help: lover of Eva Braun, confidant of Hitler, I have long been the official Jew of the Third Reich. To the end, I spend my weekends in Obersalzberg and the Nazi bigwigs show me the utmost respect.

Hilda's bedroom was on the top floor of a grand old townhouse on Backerstraße. The room was remarkable for its spaciousness, its high ceilings, a four poster bed, a picture window. In the middle, a cage with a Jewish nightingale. In one corner, a wooden horse. Here and there, a number of kaleidoscopes. Each stamped 'Schlemilovitch Ltd., New York'.

'Probably a Jew,' Hilda confided, 'but he makes beautiful kaleidoscopes. I adore kaleidoscopes. Look in this one, Raphäel! A human face made up of a thousand brilliant facets constantly shifting . . .'

I want to confess to her that my father was responsible for these miniature works of art, but she constantly kvetches to me about the Jews. They demand compensation on the pretext that their families were exterminated in the camps, they are bleeding Germany white. They drove around in Mercedes drinking champagne while the poor

___
* Himmler

98

Germans were working to rebuild their country and living hand-to-mouth. Oh, the bastards! First they corrupted Germany, now they were pimping it.

The Jews had won the war, had killed her father, raped her mother, her position was unshakeable. Better to wait a few days before showing her my family tree. Until then, I would be the epitome of Gallic charm: the Grey Musketeers, the insolence, the elegance, the *made in Paris* spirit. Had not Hilda complimented me on the mellifluent way I spoke French?

'Never,' she would say, 'never have I heard a Frenchman speak his mother tongue as beautifully as you.'

'I'm from Touraine,' I explained. 'We pride ourselves on speaking the purest French. My name is Raphäel de Château-Chinon, but don't tell anyone. I swallowed my passport so I could remain incognito. One more thing: as a good Frenchman, I find Austrian food DIS-GUS-TING! When I think of the *canards à l'orange*, the nuits-saint-georges, the sauternes and the *poularde de Bresse*! Hilda, I will take you to France, knock some of the rough edges off you. *Vive la France*, Hilda! You people are savages!'

She tried to make me forget Austro-German uncouthness, talking to me about Mozart, Schubert. Hugo von Hofmannsthal.

'Hofmannsthal?' I said, 'A Jew, my little Hilda! Austria is a Jewish colony. Freud, Zweig, Schnitzler, Hofmannsthal, it's a ghetto! I defy you to name me a great Tyrolean poet! In France, we don't allow ourselves to be overrun like that. The likes of Montaigne and Proust and Louis-Ferdinand Céline have never succeeded in Jewifying our country. Ronsard and Du Bellay are there, keeping an eye open for any trouble! In fact, my little Hilda, we French make no distinction between Germans, Austrians, Czechs, Hungarians and all the other Jews. And don't talk to me about your papa, SS Murzzuschlag, or the Nazis. All Jews, *meine kleine* Hilda, the Nazis are the shock troops of the Jews! Think about Hitler, the little runt of a corporal wandering the streets of Vienna, beaten, numb with cold, starving to death! Long live Hitler!'

She listened to me, her eyes wide. Soon I would tell her more brutal truths. I would reveal my identity. I would choose the perfect moment and whisper into her ear the confession the nameless knight made to the Inquisitor's daughter:

Ich, Señora, eur Geliebter,
Bin der Sohn des vielbelobten,
Großen, schriftgelehrten Rabbi
Israel von Saragossa.

Hilda had obviously never read Heine's poem.

In the evenings, we would often go to the Prater. I love funfairs.

'The thing is, Hilda,' I explained, 'funfairs are terribly sad. The "enchanted river", for example, you get into a boat with your friends, you are carried along by the current and when you come to the end you get a bullet in the back of the head. Then there's the House of Mirrors, the roller-coaster, the merry-go-rounds, the shooting galleries. You stand in front of the distorting mirrors and your emaciated face, your skeletal chest terrify you. The cars on the roller-coaster systematically derail and you break your back. The merry-go-rounds are surrounded by archers who shoot little poisoned darts into your spine. The merry-go-round never stops, victims fall from the wooden horses. From time to time, the machinery seizes up, clogged with piles of corpses and the archers clear the area for the newcomers. Passers-by are encouraged to stand in little groups inside the shooting galleries. The archers are told to aim between the eyes, but sometimes an arrow goes wide and hits an ear, an eye, a gaping mouth. When they hit their mark, the archers are awarded five points. When the arrow goes astray, five points are deducted. The archer with the highest score wins a young blonde Pomeranian girl, an ornament made of silver paper and a chocolate skull. I forgot to mention the lucky bags at the sweet stalls: every bag sold contains a few amethyst blue crystals of cyanide, with instructions for use: "*Na, friss schon!*"* Bags

---

* 'Go on, eat up!'

of cyanide for everyone. Six million of them! We're happy here in Theresienstadt . . .'

Next to the Prater is a large park where lovers stroll; in the gathering dark I led Hilda under the leafy boughs, next to the banks of flowers, the blue-tinged lawns. I slapped her three times. It gave me pleasure to watch blood trickle from the corners of her mouth. Great pleasure. A German girl. Who once had loved an SS Totenkopf. I know how to bear an old grudge.

Now, I let myself slip down the slope of confession. I look nothing like Gregory Peck as I claimed earlier. I have neither the energy nor the *keep smiling* spirit of the American. I look like my cousin, the Jewish painter Modigliani. They called him 'The Tuscan Christ'. I forbid the use of this moniker to refer to my handsome tubercular face.

But actually, no, I look no more like Modigliani than I do like Gregory Peck. I'm the spitting image of Groucho Marx: the same eyes, the same nose, the same moustache. Worse still, I'm a dead ringer for Süss the Jew. Hilda had to notice at all costs. For a week now, she had not been firm enough with me.

Lying around her room were recordings of the 'Horst-Wessel-Lied' and the 'Hitlerleute' which she kept in memory of her father. The vultures of Stalingrad and the phosphorus of Hamburg will eat away at the vocal cords of these warriors. Everyone's turn comes eventually. I bought two record-players. To compose my *Judeo-Nazi Requiem*, I simultaneously played the 'Horst-Wessel-Lied' and the 'Einheitsfrontlied' of the International Brigades. Next I blended the 'Hitlerleute' with the anthem of the Thälmann-Kolonne, the last cry of Jews and German communists. And then, at the end of the *Requiem*, Wagner's *Götterdämmerung* conjured Berlin in flames, the tragic destiny of the German people, while the litany for the dead of Auschwitz evoked the pounds into which six million dogs were hurled.

Hilda does not work. I inquire about the source of her income. She explains that she sold some Biedermeier furniture belonging to a dead aunt for twenty thousand *schillings*. Barely a quarter of that sum is left.

I tell her my concerns.

'Don't worry, Raphäel,' she says.

Every night she goes to the Blaue Bar at the Hotel Sacher. She seeks out the most well-heeled guests and sells them her charms. After three weeks, we have fifteen hundred dollars. Hilda develops a taste for the profession. It offers her a discipline and a stability she has not had until now.

She artlessly makes the acquaintance of Yasmine. This young woman also haunts the Hotel Sacher offering her dark eyes, her bronzed skin, her oriental languor to Americans passing through.

At first, they compare notes on their profession, and quickly become the best of friends. Yasmine moves in to Backerstraße, the four-poster bed is big enough for three.

Of the two women in your harem, these two charming whores, Yasmine quickly became your favourite. She talks to you of Istanbul, where she was born, of the Galata Bridge, the Valide Mosque. You feel a sudden urge to reach the Bosphorus. In Vienna, winter is drawing in and you will not make it out alive. When the first snows began to fall, you clung more tightly to your Turkish friend. You left Vienna and visited cousins who manufactured playing cards in Trieste. From there, a brief detour to Budapest. No cousins left in Budapest. Exterminated. In Salonika, the birthplace of your family, you discovered the same desolation, the Jewish community of this city had been of particular interest to the Germans. In Istanbul, your cousins Sarah, Rachel, Dinah and Blanca celebrated the return of the prodigal son. You rediscovered your taste for life and for *lokum*. Already, your cousins in Cairo were waiting impatiently for you to visit. They asked for news of your exiled cousins in London, in Paris, in Caracas.

You spent some time in Egypt. Since you did not have a penny to your name, you organised a funfair in Port Said with all your old friends as exhibits. For twenty dinars a head, passers-by could watch Hitler in a cage declaiming Hamlet's soliloquy, Göring and Rudolph Hess on the trapeze, Himmler and his performing dogs, Goebbels the snake charmer, von Schirach the sword swallower, Julius Streicher the wandering Jew. Some distance away, the 'Collabo's Beauties' were performing an improvised

'Oriental' revue: there was Robert Brasillach dressed as a sultan, Drieu la Rochelle as the *bayadère*, Albert Bonnard as the guardian of the seraglio, Bonny and Lafton the bloodthirsty viziers and the missionary Mayol de Lupé. The 'Vichy Follies' singers were performing an operetta extravaganza: among the troupe were a Maréchal, admirals Esteva, Bard and Platón, a few bishops, brigadier Darnand and the traitorous Prince Laval. Even so, the most visited stall in the fairground was the one where people stripped your former mistress Eva Braun. She was still a handsome woman. For a hundred dinars each, aficionados could find out for themselves.

After a week, you abandoned your cherished ghosts and left with the takings. You crossed the Red Sea, reached Palestine and died of exhaustion. And there you were, you had made it all the way from Paris to Jerusalem.

Between them, my two girlfriends earned three thousand *schillings* a night. Prostitution and pandering suddenly seemed to me to be ill-paid professions unless practised on the scale of a Lucky Luciano. Unfortunately, I was not cast from the same mould as that captain of industry.

Yasmine introduced me to a number of dubious individuals: Jean-Farouk de Mérode, Paulo Hayakawa, the ageing Baroness Lydia Stahl, Sophie Knout, Rachid von Rosenheim, M. Igor, T.W.A. Levy, Otto da Silva and others whose names I've forgotten. With these shady characters, I trafficked gold, laundered counterfeit zlotys and sold wild grasses like hashish and marijuana to anyone who wished to graze on them. Eventually I enlisted in the French Gestapo. Badge number S. 1113. Working from the Rue Lauriston.

I had been bitterly disappointed by the *Milice*. There, the only people I had met were boy scouts just like the brave lads in the Résistance. Darnand was an out-and-out idealist.

I felt more comfortable around Pierre Bonny, Henri Chamberlin-Lafont and their acolytes. What's more, on the Rue Lauriston I met up with my old ethics teacher, Joseph Joanovici.

To the killers in the Gestapo, Joano and I were the two in-house Jews. The third was in Hamburg. His name was Maurice Sachs.

One tires of everything. In the end I left my two girl-friends and the merry little band of crooks who jeopardised my health. I followed an avenue as far as the Danube. It was dark, snow was falling benignly. Would I throw myself into the river or not? Franz-Josefs-Kai was deserted, from somewhere I could hear snatches of a song, 'Weisse Weihnacht', ah yes, people were celebrating Christmas. Miss Evelyn used to read me Dickens and Andersen. What joy the next morning to find thousands of toys at the foot of the tree. All this happened in the house on the Quai Conti, on the banks of the Seine. An exceptional childhood, a magical childhood I no longer have time to tell you about. An elegant swan dive into the Danube on Christmas Eve? I was sorry I had not left a farewell note for Hilda and Yasmine. For example: 'I will not be home tonight, for the night will be black and white.' No matter. I consoled myself with the thought that these two whores had probably never read Gérard de Nerval. Thankfully, in Paris, no one would fail to see the link between Nerval and Schlemilovitch, the two winter suicides. I was incorrigible. I was prepared to appropriate another man's death just as I had appropriated the pens of Proust and Céline, the paintbrushes of Modigliani and Soutine, the gurning faces of Groucho Marx and Chaplin. My tuberculosis? Had I not stolen it from Franz Kafka? I could still change my mind and die like him in the Kierling sanatorium not far from here. Nerval or Kafka? Suicide or sanatorium? No, suicide did not suit me, a Jew has no right to commit suicide. Such luxury should be left to Werther. What then? Turn up at Kierling sanatorium? Could I be sure that I would die there, like Kafka?

I did not hear him approach. He brusquely shoves a badge into my face on which I read POLIZEI. He asks for my papers. I've forgotten them. He takes me by the arm. I ask him why he does not use his handcuffs. He gives a reassuring little laugh.

'Now, now, sir, you've had too much to drink. The Christmas spirit, probably. Come on now, I'll take you home. Where do you live?'

I obstinately refuse to give him my address.

'Well, in that case I have no choice but to take you to the station.'

The apparent kindness of the policeman is getting on my nerves. I've already worked out that he belongs to the Gestapo. Why not just tell me straight out? Maybe he thinks I will put up a fight, scream like a stuck pig? Not at all. Kierling sanatorium is no match for the clinic where this good man plans to take me. First, there will be the customary formalities: I will be asked for my surname, my first name, my date of birth. They will ensure I am genuinely ill, force me to take some sinister test. Next, the operating theatre. Lying on the table, I will wait impatiently for my surgeons Torquemada and Ximénes. They will hand me an x-ray of my lungs which I will see are nothing but a mass of hideous tumours like the tentacles of an octopus.

'Do you wish us to operate or not?' Dr Torquemada will ask me calmly.

'All we need do is transplant two stainless steel lungs,' Dr Ximénes will gently explain.

'We have a superior professional conscientiousness,' Dr Torquemada will say.

'Together with an acute interest in your health,' said Dr Ximénes.

'Unfortunately, most of our patients love their illness with a fierce passion and consequently see us not as surgeons . . .'

' . . . but as torturers.'

'Patients are often unjust towards their doctors,' Dr Ximénes will add.

'We are forced to treat them against their will,' Dr Torquemada will say.

'A thankless task,' Dr Ximénes will add.

'Do you know that some patients in our clinic have formed a union?' Dr Torquemada will ask me. 'They have decided to strike, to refuse to allow us to treat them . . .'

'A serious threat to the medical profession,' Dr Ximénes will add. 'Especially since the unionist fever is infecting all sectors of the clinic . . .'

'We have tasked a very scrupulous practitioner, Dr Himmler, to crush this rebellion. He is systematically performing euthanasia on all the union members.'

'So what do you decide . . .' Dr Torquemada will ask me, 'the operation or euthanasia?'

'There are no other possible alternatives.'

Events did not unfold as I had expected. The policeman was still holding my arm, telling me he was walking me to the nearest police station for a simple identity check. When I stepped into his office, the Kommissar, a cultured SS officer intimately familiar with the French poets, asked:

'Say, what have you done, you who come here, with your youth?'

I explained to him how I had wasted it. And then I talked to him about my impatience: at an age when others were planning their future, I could think only of ending things. Take the gare de Lyon, for example, under the German occupation. I was supposed to catch a train that would carry me far away from misfortune and fear. Travellers were queuing at the ticket desks. I had only to wait half an hour to get my ticket. But no, I got into a first class carriage without a ticket like an imposter. At Chalon-sur-Saône, when the German ticket inspectors checked the compartment, they caught me. I held out my hands. I told them that despite the false papers in the name Jean Cassis de Coudray Macouard, I was a JEW. The relief!

'Then they brought me to you, Herr Kommissar. You decide my fate. I promise I will be utterly docile.'

The Kommissar smiles gently, pats my cheek and asks whether I really have tuberculosis.

'It doesn't surprise me,' he says. 'At your age, everyone is consumptive. It needs to be treated, otherwise you end up spitting blood and dragging yourself along all your life. This is what I've decided: if you'd been born earlier, I would have sent you to Auschwitz to have your tuberculosis treated, but we live in more civilised times. Here, this is a ticket for Israel. Apparently, over there, the Jews . . .'

The sea was inky blue and Tel Aviv was white, so white. As the boat came alongside, the steady beat of his heart made him feel he had returned to his ancestral land after two thousand years away. He had embarked at Marseille, with the Israeli national shipping line. All through the crossing, he tried to calm his rising panic by anaesthetising himself with alcohol and morphine. Now, with Tel Aviv spread out before him, he could die, his heart at peace.

The voice of Admiral Levy roused him from his thoughts.

'Good crossing, young man? First time in Israel? You'll love our country. A terrific country, you'll see. Lads of your age are swept up by the extraordinary energy that, from Haifa to Eilat, from Tel Aviv to the Dead Sea . . .'

'I'm sure you're right, Admiral.'

'Are you French? We have a great love of France, the liberal traditions, the warmth of Anjou and Touraine, the scents of Provence. And your national anthem, it's beautiful! "*Allons enfants de la patrie!*" Capital, capital!'

'I'm not entirely French, Admiral, I am a French JEW. A French JEW.'

Admiral Levy gave him a hostile glare. Admiral Levy looks like the twin brother of Admiral Dönitz. After a moment Admiral Levy says curtly:

'Follow me, please.'

He ushers the young man into a sealed cabin.

'I advise you to be sensible. We will deal with you in due course.'

The admiral switches off the electricity and double locks the door.

He sat in total darkness for almost three hours. Only the faint glow of his wristwatch still connected him to the world. The door was flung open and his eyes were dazzled by the bare bulb dangling from the ceiling. Three men in green oilskins strode towards him. One of them held out a card.

'Elias Bloch, Secret State Police. You're a French Jew? Excellent! Put him in handcuffs!'

A fourth stooge, wearing an identical trench coat, stepped into the cabin.

'A very productive search. In the gentleman's luggage we found several books by Proust and Kafka, reproductions of Modigliani and Soutine, some photos of Charlie Chaplin, Erich von Stroheim and Groucho Marx.'

'Your case is looking more and more serious,' says the man named Elias Bloch. 'Take him away!'

The men bundle him out of the cabin. The handcuffs chafe his wrists. On the quayside, he tripped and fell down. One of the officers takes the opportunity to give him a few swift kicks in the ribs then, grabbing the chain linking the handcuffs, dragged him to his feet. They crossed the deserted docks. A police van exactly like the ones used by the French police in the roundup on 16 July 1942 was parked on the street corner. Elias Bloch slid into the seat next to the driver. The young man climbed into the back followed by three officers.

The police van sets off up the Champs-Élysées. People are queuing outside the cinemas. On the terrace of Fouquet's, women are wearing pale dresses. It was clearly a Saturday evening in spring.

They stopped at the Place de l'Étoile. A few GIs were photographing the Arc de Triomphe, but he felt no need to call to them for help. Bloch grabbed his arm and marched him across the *place*. The four officers followed a few paces behind.

'So, you're a French Jew?' Bloch asked, his face looming close.

He suddenly looked like Henri Chamberlin-Lafont of the Gestapo Française.

He was bundled into a black Citroën parked on the Avenue Kléber.

'You're for it now,' said the officer on his right.

'For a beating, right, Saul?' said the officer on his left.

'Yes, Isaac, he's in for a beating,' said the officer driving.

'I'll do it.'

'No, let me! I need the exercise,' said the officer on his right.

'No, Isaac! It's my turn. You got to beat the shit out of the English Jew last night. This one's mine.'

'Apparently this one's a French Jew.'

'That's weird. Why don't we call him Marcel Proust?'

Isaac gave him a brutal punch in the stomach.

'On your knees, Marcel! On your knees!'

Meekly he complied. The back seat made it difficult. Isaac slapped him six times.

'You're bleeding, Marcel: that means you're still alive.'

Saul whipped out a leather belt.

'Catch, Marcel Proust,' he said.

The belt hit him on the left cheek and he almost passed out.

'Poor little brat,' said Isaiah. 'Poor little French Jew.'

He passed the Hôtel Majestic. All the windows of the great façade were dark. To reassure himself, he decided that Otto Abetz flanked by all the jolly fellows of the Collaboration were in the lobby for him, the guest of honour at a Franco-German dinner. After all, was he not the official Jew to the Third Reich?

'We're taking you on a little tour of the area,' said Isaiah.

'There are a lot of historical monuments around here,' said Saul.

'We'll stop at each one so you have a chance to appreciate them.'

They showed him the buildings requisitioned by the Gestapo: Nos. 31 *bis* and 72 Avenue Foch. 57 Boulevard Lannes. 48 Rue de Villejust. 101 Avenue Henri-Martin. Nos. 3 and 5 Rue Mallet-Stevens. Nos. 21 and 23 Square de Bois-de-Boulogne. 25 Rue d'Astorg. 6 Rue Adolphe-Yvon. 64 Boulevard Suchet. 49 Rue de la Faisanderie. 180 Rue de la Pompe.

Having finished the sightseeing tour, they headed back to the Kléber-Boissière sector.

'So what did you make of the 16th *arrondissement*?' Isaiah asked him.

'It's the most notorious district in Paris,' said Saul.

'And now, driver, take us to 93 Rue Lauriston, please,' said Isaac.

He felt reassured. His friends Bonny and Chamberlin-Lafont would soon put an end to this tasteless joke. They would drink champagne together as they did every night. René Launay, head of the Gestapo on the Avenue Foch, 'Rudy' Martin from the Gestapo in Neuilly, Georges Delfanne from the Avenue Henri-Martin and Odicharia from the 'Georgia Gestapo' would join them. Order would be restored.

Isaac rang the bell at 93 Rue Lauriston. The building looked deserted.

'The boss is probably waiting for us at 3 *bis* Place des États-Unis for the beating,' said Isaiah.

Bloch paced up and down the pavement. He opened the door to number 3 *bis* and dragged the young man inside.

He knew this *hôtel particulier* well. His friends Bonny and Chamberlin-Lafont had remodelled the property to create eight holding cells and two torture chambers, since the premises at 93 Rue Lauriston served as the administrative headquarters.

They went up to the fourth floor. Bloch opened a window.

'The Place des États-Unis is quiet this evening,' he said. 'See how the streetlights cast a soft glow over the leaves, my young friend. A beautiful May evening. And to think, we have to torture you. The bathtub torture, as it happens. How sad. A little glass of curaçao for Dutch courage? A Craven? Or would you prefer a little music? In a while, we'll play you a little song by Charles Trenet. It will drown out your screams. The neighbours are sensitive. They prefer the voice of Trenet to the sound of you being tortured.'

Saul, Isaac and Isaiah entered. They had not taken off their green trench coats. He immediately noticed the bathtub in the middle of the room.

'It once belonged to Émilienne d'Alençon,' Bloch said with a sad smile. 'Admire the quality of the enamelling, my friend, the floral motifs, the platinum taps.'

Isaac wrenched his hands behind his back while Isaiah put on the handcuffs. Saul turned on the phonograph. Raphäel immediately recognised the voice of Charles Trenet:

Formidable,
J'entends le vent sur la mer.
Formidable
Je vois la pluie, les éclairs.
Formidable
Je sens bientôt qu'il va faire,
qu'il va faire
Un orage
Formidable . . .

Sitting on the window ledge, Bloch beat time.

They plunged my head into the freezing water. My lungs felt as though they might explode at any minute. The faces I had loved flashed past. The faces of my mother and my father. My old French teacher Adrien Debigorre. The face of Fr. Perrache. The face of Colonel Aravis. And then the faces of all my wonderful fiancées – I had one in every province. Bretagne, Normandy, Poitou. Corrèze. Lozère. Savoie . . . Even one in Limousin. In Bellac. If these thugs spared my life, I would write a wonderful novel: *Schlemilovitch and the Limousin*, in which I would show that I am a perfectly assimilated Jew.

They yanked me by the hair. I heard Charles Trenet again:

> . . . *Formidable.*
> *On se croirait au ciné-*
> *Matographe*
> *Où l'on voit tant de belles choses,*
> *Tant de trucs, de métamorphoses,*
> *Quand une rose*
> *est assassinée . . .*

'The second dunking will last longer,' Bloch explains wiping away a tear.

This time, two hands press down on my neck, two more on the back of my head. Before I drown, it occurs to me I have not always been kind to maman.

But they drag me back into the fresh air.

> *Et puis*
> *et puis*
> *sur les quais,*
> *la pluie*
> *la pluie*
> *n'a pas compliqué*
> *la vie*
> *qui rigole*
> *et qui se mire dans les flaques des rigoles.*

'Now let's get down to business,' says Bloch, stifling a sob.

They lay me on the floor. Isaac takes a Swiss penknife from his pocket and makes deep slashes in the soles of my feet. Then he orders me to walk across a heap of salt. Next, Saul conscientiously rips out three of my fingernails. Then, Isaiah files down my teeth. At that point Trenet was singing:

> *Quel temps*
> *pour les p'tits poissons.*
> *Quel temps*
> *pour les grands garçons.*
> *Quel temps*
> *pour les tendrons.*
> *Mesdemoiselles nous vous attendrons . . .*

'I think that's enough for tonight,' said Elias Bloch, shooting me a tender look.

He stroked my chin.

'This is the prison for the foreign Jews,' he said, 'we'll take you to the cell for French Jews. You're the only one at the moment. But there will be more along soon. Don't you worry.'

'The little shits can sit around talking about Marcel Proust,' said Isaiah.

'When I hear the word culture, I reach for my truncheon,' said Saul.

'I get to deliver the *coup de grâce*!' said Isaac.

'Come now, don't frighten the young man,' Bloch said imploringly.

He turned to me.

'Tomorrow, you will be advised about the progress of your case.'

Isaac and Saul pushed me into a little room. Isaiah came in and handed me a pair of striped pyjamas. Sewn onto the pyjama jacket was a yellow star of David on which I read *Französisch Jude*. As he closed the reinforced door, Isaac tripped me and I fell flat on my face.

The cell was illuminated by a nightlight. It did not take me long to notice the floor was strewn with Gillette Extra-Blue blades. How had the police known about my vice, my uncontrollable urge to swallow razor blades? I was sorry now that they had not chained me to the wall. All night, I had to tense myself, to bite my hand so as not to give in to the urge. One false move and I was in danger of gulping down the blades one by one. Gorging myself on Gillette Extra-Blues. It was truly the torment of Tantalus.

In the morning, Isaiah and Isaac came to fetch me. We walked down an endless corridor. Isaiah gestured to a door and told me to go in. Isaac thumped me on the back of the head by way of goodbye.

He was sitting at a large mahogany desk. Apparently, he was expecting me. He was wearing a black uniform and I noticed two Stars of David on the lapel of his jacket. He was smoking a pipe, which gave him a more pronounced jawline. Had he been wearing a beret, he might have passed for Joseph Darnand.

'You are Raphäel Schlemilovitch?' he asked in a clipped, military tone.

'Yes.'

'French Jew?'

'Yes.'

'You were arrested last night by Admiral Levy aboard the ship *Zion*?'

'Yes.'

'And handed over to the police authorities, to Commandant Elias Bloch to be specific?'

'Yes.'

'And these seditious pamphlets were found in your luggage?'

He passed me a volume of Proust, Franz Kafka's *Diary*, the photographs of Chaplin, von Stroheim and Groucho Marx, the reproductions of Modigliani and Soutine.

'Very well, allow me to introduce myself: General Tobie Cohen, Commissioner for Youth and Raising Morale. Now, let's get straight to the point. Why did you come to Israel?'

'I'm a romantic by nature. I didn't want to die without having seen the land of my forefathers.'

'And you are intending to RETURN to Europe, are you not? To go back to this playacting, this farce of yours?

Don't bother to answer, I've heard it all before: Jewish angst, Jewish misery, Jewish fear, Jewish despair . . . People wallow in their misfortunes, they ask for more, they want to go back to the comfortable world of the ghettos, the delights of the pogroms. There are two possibilities, Schlemilovitch: either you listen to me and you follow my instructions, in that case, everything will be fine. Or you continue to play the rebel, the wandering Jew, the martyr, in which case I hand you over to Commandant Elias Bloch. You know what Elias Bloch will do with you?'

'Yes, sir!'

'I warn you, we have all the means necessary to subdue little masochists like you,' he said, wiping away a tear. 'Last week, an English Jew tried to outsmart us. He turned up from Europe with the same old hard-luck stories: Diaspora, persecution, the tragic destiny of the Jewish people! . . . He dug his heels in, determined to play the tormented soul! He refused to listen! Right now, Bloch and his lieutenants are dealing with him! I can assure you, he will get to experience real suffering. Far beyond his wildest expectations. He is finally about to experience the tragic destiny of the Jewish people! He asked for Torquemada, demanded Himmler himself! Bloch is taking care of him! He's worth more than all the Grand Inquisitors and Gestapo officers combined. Do you really want to end up in his hands, Schlemilovitch?'

'No, sir.'

'Well then, listen to me: you have just arrived in a young, vigorous, dynamic country. From Tel Aviv to the Dead Sea, from Haifa to Eilat, no one is interested in hearing about the angst, the malaise, the tears, the HARD LUCK STORY of the Jews. No one! We don't want to hear another word about the Jewish critical thinking, Jewish intelligence, Jewish scepticism, Jewish contortions and humiliations, Jewish tragedy . . . (his face was bathed in tears.) We leave all that to callow European aesthetes like you. We are forceful people, square-jawed, pioneers, not a bunch of Yiddish *chanteuses* like Proust and Kafka and Chaplin. Let me tell you, we recently organised an auto-da-fé on Tel Aviv main square: the works of Proust, Kafka and their ilk, reproductions of Soutine, Modigliani and other invertebrates, were burned by our young people, fine boys and girls who would have been the envy of the *Hitlerjugend*: blond, blue-eyed, broad-shouldered, with a confident swagger and a taste for action and for fighting! (He groaned.) While you were off cultivating your neuroses, they were building their muscles. While you were kvetching, they were working in kibbutzim! Aren't you ashamed, Schlemilovitch?'

'Yes, sir! General, sir!'

'Good! Now promise me that you will never again read Proust, Kafka and the like or drool over reproductions of Modigliani and Soutine, or think about Chaplin or von Stroheim or the Marx Brothers, promise me you will forget

Doctor Louis-Ferdinand Céline, the most insidious Jew of all time!'

'You have my word, sir.'

'I will introduce you to fine books. I have a great quantity in French! Have you read *The Art of Leadership* by Courtois? Sauvage's *The Restoration of the Family and National Revolution*? *The Greatest Game of my Life* by Guy de Larigaudie? *The Father's Handbook* by Rear-Admiral Penfentenyo? You will learn them by heart, I plan to develop your moral muscle! For the same reason, I am sending you to a disciplinary kibbutz immediately. Don't worry, you will only be there for three months. Just enough time to build up the biceps you sorely lack and cleanse you of the germs of the cosmopolitan Jew. Is that clear?'

'Yes, sir.'

'You may go, Schlemilovitch. I'll have my orderly bring you the books I mentioned. Read them while you're waiting to go and swing a pickaxe in the Negev. Shake my hand, Schlemilovitch. Harder, man, for God's sake! Eyes front! Chin up! We'll make a sabra of you yet!' (He burst into tears.)

'Thank you, general.'

S aul led me back to my cell. He threw a few punches but my warder seemed to have mellowed considerably since the previous night. I suspected him of eavesdropping. He had doubtless been impressed by the meekness I had shown with General Cohen.

That night, Isaac and Isaiah bundled me into an army truck with a number of other young men, foreign Jews like me. They were all wearing striped pyjamas.

'No talking about Kafka, Proust and that lot,' said Isaiah.

'When we hear the word culture, we reach for our truncheons,' said Isaac.

'We're not too keen on intelligence,' said Isaiah.

'Especially when it's Jewish,' said Isaac.

'And I don't want any of you playing the martyr,' said Isaiah, 'it's gone beyond a joke. It's all very well you pulling long faces for the goyim back in Europe. But here there's just us, so don't waste your time.'

'Understood?' said Isaac. 'You will sing until we reach our destination. A few patriotic songs will do you good. Repeat after me . . .'

At about four in the afternoon, we arrived at the penal kibbutz. A huge concrete building surrounded by barbed wire. All around, the desert stretched as far as the eye could see. Isaiah and Isaac lined us up by the gates and took a roll call. There were eight of us: three English Jews, an Italian Jew, two German Jews, an Austrian Jew and me, a French Jew. The camp commandant appeared and stared at each of us in turn. The sight of this blond colossus in his black uniform did not fill me with confidence. And yet two Stars of David glittered on the lapel of his jacket.

'A bunch of intellectuals, obviously,' he roared at us furiously. 'How can I be expected to create shock troops out of this human detritus? A fine reputation you lot have made for us in Europe with your whining and your critical thinking. Well, gentlemen, here there'll be less bitching and more body building. There'll be no criticism and lots of construction! Reveille tomorrow morning at 06.00 hours. Now, up to your dormitory. Come on! Move it! Hup Two! Hup Two!'

Once we were in bed, the camp commandant strode into the dormitory followed by three young men as tall and blond as himself.

'These are your supervisors,' he said in a soft voice, 'Siegfried Levy, Günther Cohen, Hermann Rappoport. These archangels will knock you into shape! The slightest insubordination is punishable by death! Isn't that so, my darlings? Don't hesitate to shoot them if they annoy you . . . A bullet in the temple, no discussions! Understood, my angels?'

He gently stroked their cheeks.

'I don't want these European Jews undermining your moral fibre . . .'

At 06:00 hours, Siegfried, Günther and Hermann dragged us from our beds, punching us as they did so. We pulled on our striped pyjamas. They led us to the administrative office of the kibbutz. We rattled off our surnames, first names, dates of birth to a dark-haired young woman wearing the regulation army khaki shirt and grey-blue trousers. Siegfried, Günther and Hermann stood behind the office door. One after another, my companions left the room after answering the young woman's questions. My turn came. The young woman raised her head and stared me straight in the eye. She looked like the twin sister of Tania Arcisewska. She said:

'My name is Rebecca and I love you.'

I did not know how to answer.

'Listen,' she said, 'they're going to kill you. You have to leave tonight. I'll take care of everything. I'm an officer in the Israeli army so I don't have to answer to the camp commandant. I'll borrow a truck on the pretext that I have to go to Tel Aviv to attend a meeting of the chiefs of staff. You'll come with me. I'll steal Siegfried Levy's papers and give them to you. That way you won't have to worry about the police for the time being. Later, we'll see what we can do. We could take the first boat to Europe and get married. I love you, I love you! I'll have you brought to my office at eight o'clock tonight. Fall out!'

We broke rocks in the blazing sun until 5 p.m. I had never handled a pickaxe before and my pale hands were bleeding horribly. Siegfried, Günther and Hermann smoked Lucky Strikes and stood guard. At no point during the day did they utter a single word and I assumed they were mute. Siegfried raised a hand to let us know our work was finished. Hermann walked over to the three English Jews, took out his revolver and shot them, his eyes utterly expressionless. He lit a Lucky Strike and puffed on it, staring up at the sky. After summarily burying the English Jews, our three guards led us back to the kibbutz. We were left to stare out through the barbed wire at the desert. At eight o'clock, Hermann Rappoport came to fetch me and escorted me to the administrative office.

'I feel like having a little fun, Hermann!' Rebecca said. 'Leave this little Jew with me, I'll take him to Tel Aviv, rape him and kill him, promise!'

Hermann nodded.

'Well then, it's just the two of us!' she said ominously.

As soon as Rappoport left the room, she squeezed my hand affectionately.

'Follow me, we don't have a moment to lose!'

We went out through the gates and climbed into a military truck. She got behind the steering wheel.

'Freedom is ours!' she said. 'We'll stop in a little while. You can slip on Siegfried's uniform, I've just stolen it. His papers are in the inside pocket.'

We reached our destination at 11 p.m.

'I love you and I want to go back to Europe,' she told me. 'Here there's nothing but thugs, soldiers, boy scouts and *nudniks*. In Europe we'll be happy. We'll be able to read Kafka to our children.'

'Yes, my darling Rebecca. We'll dance all night and tomorrow morning we'll catch the first boat for Marseille!'

The soldiers we encountered in the street snapped to attention as Rebecca passed.

'I'm a lieutenant,' she said, smiling. 'But I can't wait to throw this uniform away and go back to Europe.'

Rebecca knew a clandestine nightclub in Tel Aviv where we danced to the songs of Zarah Leander and Marlene Dietrich. It was a very popular club among young women in the army. To gain admittance, their companions had to wear a Luftwaffe officer's uniform. The dim lighting was conducive to intimacy. Their first dance was a tango, 'Der Wind hat mir ein Lied erzählt', sung by Zarah Leander in a smouldering voice. He murmured into Rebecca's ear 'Du bist der Lenz nachdem ich verlangte.' During their second dance, 'Schön war die Zeit', he held her shoulders and kissed her passionately on the lips. The voice of Lala Andersen quickly snuffed out that of Zarah Leander. At the first words of 'Lili Marlene', they heard the police sirens. There was a great commotion but no one could get out: Commandant Elias Bloch, Saul, Isaac and Isaiah had burst into the club, waving their revolvers.

'Round up all these fools,' roared Bloch, 'but first, do a quick identity check.'

When his turn came, Bloch recognised him in spite of the Luftwaffe uniform.

'Schlemilovitch? What are you doing here? I thought you had been sent to a disciplinary kibbutz! And wearing a Luftwaffe uniform! Clearly European Jews are irredeemable.'

'Your fiancée?' He gestured to Rebecca. 'A French Jew I'm guessing? Dressed as an Israeli army officer! This just gets better and better! Look, here come my friends. Well, I'm a generous man, let's crack open a bottle of champagne!'

They were quickly surrounded by a group of revellers who clapped them on the shoulder. He recognised the Marquise de Fougeire-Jusquiames, Vicomte Lévy-Vendôme, Paulo Hayakawa, Sophie Knout, Jean-Farouk de Mérode, Otto da Silva, M. Igor, the ageing Baroness Lydia Stahl, the princess Chericheff-Deborazoff, Louis-Ferdinand Céline and Jean-Jacques Rousseau.

'I've just sold fifty thousand pairs of socks to the Wehrmacht,' announced Jean-Farouk de Mérode as they sat down.

'And I've sold ten thousand tins of paint to the Kriegsmarine,' said Otto da Silva.

'Did you know those boy scouts on Radio Londres have condemned me to death?' said Paulo Hayakawa. 'They call me the "Nazi brandy bootlegger"!'

'Don't worry,' said Lévy-Vendôme, 'we'll buy up the French *Résistants* and the Anglo-Americans the same way we bought the Germans! Always keep in mind this maxim by our master Joanovici: "I did not sell myself to the Germans. It is I, Joseph Joanovici, Jew, who BUYS Germans."'

'I've been working for the French Gestapo in Neuilly for almost a week,' said M. Igor.

'I'm the best informant in Paris,' said Sophie Knout. 'They call me Miss Abwehr.'

'I just love the Gestapo,' said the Marquise de Fougeire-Jusquiames,'they're so much more manly than everyone else.'

'You're so right,' said Princess Chericheff-Deborazoff, 'all those killers make me so *hot*.'

'There's a lot of good to be said for the German occupation,' said Jean-Farouk de Mérode, flashing a purple crocodile-skin wallet stuffed with banknotes.

'Paris is a lot calmer,' said Otto da Silva.

'The trees are blonder,' said Paulo Hayakawa.

'And you can hear the church bells,' said Lévy-Vendôme.

'I hope Germany is victorious!' said M. Igor.

'Would you care for a Lucky Strike?' asked the Marquise de Fougeire-Jusquiames, proffering a cigarette case of emerald-studded platinum. 'I get them regularly from Spain.'

'No, some champagne! Let's drink to the health of the Abwehr!' said Sophie Knout.

'And the Gestapo!' said Princess Chericheff-Deborazoff.

'A little stroll in the Bois de Boulogne?' suggested Commandant Bloch, turning toward him, 'I feel like a breath of fresh air! Your fiancée can join us. We'll meet up with our little gang on the Place de l'Étoile at midnight for a last drink!'

They found themselves outside on the Rue Pigalle. Commandant Bloch gestured to the three white Delahayes and the black Citroën parked outside the club.

'These all belong to our little gang,' he explained. 'We use the black Citroën for the round-ups. So let's take one of the Delahayes, if you don't mind. It will be more cheery.'

Saul got behind the wheel, he and Bloch sat in the front, with Isaiah, Rebecca and Isaac in the back.

'What were you doing at the Grand-Duc?' Commandant Bloch asked him. 'Don't you know the nightclub is reserved for French Gestapo officers and black market traffickers?'

As they approached the Place de l'Opéra, he noticed a large banner that read 'KOMMANDANTUR PLATZ'.

'How glorious to be riding in a Delahaye,' said Bloch, 'especially in Paris in May 1943. Don't you agree, Schlemilovitch?'

He stared at him intently. His eyes were kindly and compassionate.

'Let's make quite sure we understand one another, Schlemilovitch, I have no wish to thwart your vocation. Thanks to me, you will almost certainly be awarded the Martyr's Palm you've aspired to since the day you were born. Oh yes, a little later, I plan to personally give you the greatest gift you could wish for: a bullet in the back of the neck! Beforehand, we will eliminate your fiancée. Happy?'

To ward off his fear, he gritted his teeth and summoned his memories. His love affairs with Eva Braun and Hilda Murzzuschlag. His first strolls through Paris, summer 1940, in his SS Brigadenführer uniform: this was the dawn of a new era, they were going to cleanse the world, cure it forever of the Jewish plague. They had clear heads and blond hair. Later, his Panzer crushes the meadows of the Ukraine. Later still, here he is with Field Marshal Rommel striding through the desert sands. He is wounded in Stalingrad. The phosphorus bombs in Hamburg will do the rest. He followed the Führer to the last. Is he going to let himself be intimidated by Elias Bloch?

'A burst of lead in the back of the head! What do you say, Schlemilovitch?'

The eyes of commandant Bloch are on him again.

'You're one of the ones who takes his beating with a sad smile! A true Jew, the genuine, hundred per cent, *made in Europa* Jews.'

They turned into the Bois de Boulogne.

He remembers afternoons spent at the Pré-Catelan and the Grande Cascade under the watchful eye of Miss Evelyn but he will not bore you with his childhood. Read Proust, that would be best.

Saul stopped the Delahaye in the middle of the Allée des Acacias. He and Isaac dragged Rebecca out and raped her in front of my very eyes. Commandant Bloch had already handcuffed me and the car doors were locked. It hardly mattered, I would not have lifted a finger to protect my fiancée.

We drove towards the château de Bagatelle. Isaiah, more sophisticated than his two companions, gripped Rebecca by the throat and forced his penis into my fiancée's mouth. Commandant Bloch gently stabbed me in the thighs with a dagger and before long my immaculate SS uniform was drenched with blood.

Then the Delahaye stopped at the junction near Les Cascades. Isaiah and Isaac dragged Rebecca from the car again. Isaac grabbed her hair and tugged her head back. Rebecca started to laugh. The laugh grew louder, echoing around the woods, grew louder still until it reached a dizzying height and splintered into sobs.

'Your fiancée has been liquidated,' whispers Commandant Bloch, 'don't be sad. We have to get back to our friends!'

And indeed the whole gang is waiting for us on the Place de l'Étoile.

'It's after curfew,' says Jean-Farouk de Mérode, 'but we have specially-issued *Ausweise*.'

'Why don't we go to the One-Two-Two,' suggests Paulo Hayakawa. 'They have sensational girls there. No need to pay. I just have to flash my French Gestapo card.'

'Why don't we conduct a few impromptu searches of the bigwigs in the neighbourhood?' says M. Igor.

'I'd rather loot a jeweller's,' says Otto da Silva.

'Or an antiques shop,' says Lévy-Vendôme. 'I've promised Göring three *Directoire* desks.'

'What do you say to a raid?' asks Commandant Bloch. 'I know a hideout of *Résistants* on the Rue Lepic.'

'Wonderful idea!' cries Princess Chericheff-Deborazoff. 'We can torture them in my *hôtel particulier* on the Place d'Iéna.'

'We are the kings of Paris,' says Paulo Hayakawa.

'Thanks to our German friends,' says M. Igor.

'Let's have fun!' says Sophie Knout. 'We're protected by the Abwehr and the Gestapo.'

'*Après nous le déluge!*' says the Marquise de Fougeire-Jusquiames.

'Why not come down to the Rue Lauriston,' says Bloch, 'I've just had three cases of whisky delivered. Let's end the evening with a flourish.'

'You're right, commandant,' says Paulo Hayakawa, 'after all, they don't call us the Rue Lauriston Gang for nothing.'

'RUE LAURISTON! RUE LAURISTON!' chant the Marquise de Fougeire-Jusquiames and the Princess Chericheff-Deborazoff.

'No point taking the cars,' says Jean-Farouk de Mérode, 'we can walk there.'

Up to this point, they have been kind to me, but no sooner do we turn into the Rue Lauriston than they turn and glare at me in a manner that is unbearable.

'Who are you?' demands Paulo Hayakawa.

'An agent with the Intelligence Service,' says Sophie Knout.

'Explain yourself,' says Otto da Silva.

'I don't much care for that ugly mug of yours,' declares the elderly Baroness Lydia Stahl.

'Why are you dressed as an SS officer?' Jean-Farouk de Mérode asks me.

'Show me your papers,' orders M. Igor.

'Are you a Jew?' asks Lévy-Vendôme. 'Come on, confess!'

'Who do you think you are, you little thug, Marcel Proust?' inquires the Marquise de Fougeire-Jusquiames.

'He'll tell us what we want to know in the end,' declares Princess Chericheff-Devorazoff. '*Tongues are loosened at Rue Lauriston.*'

Bloch puts the handcuffs on me again. The others question me with renewed vigour. I feel a sudden urge to vomit. I lean against a doorway.

'We don't have time to waste,' says Isaac. 'March!'

'Make an effort,' says Commandant Bloch, 'we'll soon be there. It's at number 93.'

I stumble and collapse on the pavement. They encircle me. Jean-Farouk de Mérode, Paulo Hayakawa, M. Igor,

Otto da Silva and Lévy-Vendôme are all wearing striking pink evening suits and fedoras. Bloch, Isaiah, Isaac, and Saul are more austere in their green trench coats. The Marquise de Fougeire-Jusquiames, Princess Chericheff-Devorazoff, Sophie Knout and the elderly Baroness Lydia Stahl are each wearing a white mink and a diamond rivière.

Paulo Hayakawa is smoking a cigar and casually flicking the ash in my face, Princess Chericheff-Devorazoff is playfully jabbing my cheeks with her stiletto heels.

'Aren't you going to get up, Marcel Proust?' asks the Marquise de Fougeire-Jusquiames.

'Come on, Schlemilovitch,' Commandant Bloch implores me. 'We only have to cross the street. Look, there's number 93 . . .'

'He is an obstinate young man,' says Jean-Farouk de Mérode. 'If you'll excuse me, I'm going to drink a whisky. I can't bear to be parched.'

He crosses the road, followed by Paulo Hayakawa, Otto da Silva and M. Igor. The door to number 93 closes behind them.

Sophie Knout, the elderly Baroness Lydia Stahl, Princess Chericheff-Devorazoff, and the Marquise de Fougeire-Jusquiames quickly join them. The Marquise de Fougeire-Jusquiames wraps her mink coat around me, whispering in my ear:

'This will be your shroud. Adieu, my angel.'

This leaves Bloch, Isaac, Saul, Isaiah and Lévy-Vendôme. Isaac tries to haul me to my feet, tugging on the chain connecting the handcuffs.

'Leave him,' says Commandant Bloch, 'he's better lying down.'

Saul, Isaac, Isaiah and Lévy-Vendôme go and sit on the steps outside number 93. They stare at me and weep.

'I'll join the others a little later,' Commandant Bloch says to me in a sad voice. '*The whisky and champagne will flow as usual on Rue Lauriston.*'

He brings his face close to mine. He really is the spitting image of my old friend Henri Chamberlin-Lafont.

'You are going to die in an SS uniform,' he says. 'You are touching, Schlemilovitch, very touching.'

From the windows of number 93, I hear a burst of laughter and the chorus of a song:

Moi, j'aime le music-hall
Ses jongleurs
Ses danseuses légères . . .

'Hear that?' asks Bloch, his eyes misted with tears. 'In France, everything ends with a song, Schlemilovitch! So keep your spirits up!'

From the right-hand pocket of his trench coat, he takes a revolver. I struggle to my feet and stagger back. Commandant Bloch does not take his eyes off me. Sitting on the steps opposite, Isaiah, Saul, Isaac and Lévy-Vendôme are still sobbing. I consider the façade of number 93 for a moment. From the windows Jean-Farouk de Mérode, Paulo Hayakawa, M. Igor, Otto da Silva, Sophie Knout, the elderly Baroness Lydia Stahl, the Marquise de Fougeire-Jusquiames, Princess Chericheff-Devorazoff, Inspector Bonny pull faces and thumb their noses at me. A sort of cheerful sadness washes over me, one I know only too well. Rebecca was right to laugh a while ago. I summon my last ounce of strength. A nervous, feeble laugh. Gradually it swells until it shakes my whole body, doubling me over. It hardly matters that Commandant Bloch is slowly coming towards me, I feel utterly at ease. He waves his revolver and roars:

'You're laughing? YOU'RE LAUGHING? Well, take that you little Jew, take that!'

My head explodes, but I do not know whether from the bullets or from my delirious joy.

The blue walls of the room and the window. By my bed sits Sigmund Freud. To make sure I'm not dreaming, I reach out my right hand and stroke his bald pate.

' . . . my nurses picked you up on the Franz-Josefs-Kai tonight and brought you to my clinic here in Pötzleinsdorf. A course of psychoanalysis will clarify things in my mind. You'll soon be a healthy, optimistic, sporty young man, I promise. Here, I want you to read this insightful essay by your compatriot Jean-Paul Schweitzer de la Sarthe: *Anti-Semite and Jew*. There is one thing you must understand at all costs. THE JEW DOES NOT EXIST, as Schweitzer de la Sarthe so aptly puts it. YOU ARE NOT A JEW, you are a man among other men, that is all. You are not a Jew, as I have just said, you are suffering from delusions, hallucinations, fantasies, nothing more, a slight touch of paranoia . . . No one wishes you harm, my boy, all people want is to be kind to you. We are living in a world at peace. Himmler is dead, how can you remember all these things? You were not even born, come now, be reasonable, I beg you, I implore you, I . . .'

I am no longer listening to Dr Freud. And yet he goes down on his knees, arms outstretched, he pleads with me, takes his head in his hands, rolls on the floor in despair, crawls on all fours, barks, begs me again to let go of my 'hallucinatory delusions', my 'Jewish neuroses', my 'Yiddish paranoia'. I am astonished to see him in such a state: does he find my presence so disturbing?

'Stop the gesticulating.' I say. 'The only doctor I will allow to treat me is Dr Bardamu, Louis-Ferdinand Bardamu . . . A Jew like me . . . Bardamu. Louis-Ferdinand Bardamu . . .'

I got up and walked with some difficulty to the window. The psychoanalyst lay sobbing in a corner. Outside, the Pötzleinsdorfer Park was glittering with snow and sunlight. A red tram was coming down the avenue. I thought about the future being offered me: a swift cure thanks to the tender mercies of Dr Freud, men and women waiting for me at the entrance to the clinic, their expressions warm and friendly. The world, full of amazing ventures, a hive of activity.

The beautiful Pötzleinsdorfer Park, there, close by, the greenness and the sunlit pathways.

Furtively, I slip behind the psychoanalyst and pat his head.

'I'm so tired,' I tell him, 'so tired . . .'

NOTES ON *LA PLACE DE L'ÉTOILE*

1 **Léon Rabatête:** a thinly disguised parody of Lucien Rebatet (1903–1972), a French author, journalist, and intellectual; an exponent of fascism and virulent anti-Semite.

1 **Ferdinand Bardamu:** a character in Céline's *Voyage au bout de la Nuit*. Modiano calls him Doctor Louis-Ferdinand Bardamu, echoing Céline's title and first names. The first pages of the novel are a parody of the anti-Semitic tracts Céline wrote and published.

2 **Stay strong, Madelon:** a reference to the popular French WWI song 'La Madelon' (aka 'Quand Madelon') about an innkeeper's daughter who flirts with everyone but sleeps with no one.

2 **Cahen d'Anvers:** Louis Raphaël Cahen d'Anvers (1837–1922), French banker, scion of two wealthy Jewish banking families.

3 **I was compared to Barnabooth:** a reference to the title character in Valery Larbaud's novel *The Diary of A.O. Barnabooth* whose story mirrors that of our hero's 'Venezuelan inheritance'.

4 **'Laversine' ... 'Porfirio Rubirosa':** all references to the polo. Porfirio Rubirosa was a famous Dominican polo player; Cibao-La Pampa, the team he founded; the Coupe Laversine is a celebrated tournament; Silver Leys is a polo club in the UK.

5 **three photos taken by Lipnitzki:** Boris Lipnitzky (1887–1971), famous Ukrainian–French photographer.

6 **Jean-François Des Essarts:** the name deliberately echoes that of Jean des Esseintes in Huysmans' novel *À Rebours*. Modiano's character is based on Roger Nimier, the founder of the literary movement 'les Hussards'.

9 **The Finaly Affair:** Robert and Gérald Finaly, two Jewish children born in Vichy France, were taken in by a member of the Catholic network when their parents were arrested. After the war, the woman refused to return the orphaned children, whose parents had died in the camps, and illicitly had the children baptised in 1948. A national scandal ensued, which involved Cardinal Pierre-Marie Gerlier and Abbé Roger

Etchegaray. The children were finally reunited with Jewish relatives in Israel in 1953.

9 *francisques*: 'double-bladed fasces' – the fascist emblem of the Vichy regime.

9 **PPF:** Parti Populaire Français, a French fascist and Nazi political party led by Jacques Doriot before and during the Second World War.

10 **'Saint Jacob X: Actor and Martyr':** a reference to Jean-Paul Sartre's *Saint Genet, Actor and Martyr*.

10 **'La Casquette du père Bugeaud':** a French military song.

11 **Maurice Sachs (1906–45):** (born Maurice Ettinghausen) French writer. The son of a Jewish family of jewellers, he converted to Catholicism in 1925. During the war, he extorted money from Jews to help them flee the Unoccupied Zone and may have been a Gestapo informer. He was later imprisoned and died during the long march from Fuhlsbüttel prison in 1945.

11 **Lola Montès:** the title of a Max Ophüls film which was based loosely on the life of the nineteenth-century dancer Lola Montez.

12 **Le Boeuf sur le Toit:** a famous Parisian nightclub.

12 **Drieu la Rochelle (1893–1945):** French novelist and essayist, la Rochelle was a leading proponent of French fascism in the 1930s, and a collaborationist during the Nazi occupation. After the liberation of Paris in 1944, he went into hiding and committed suicide later that year.

13 **Night and fog:** a reference to *Nuit et Brouillard*, the 1955 French holocaust documentary by Alain Resnais.

13 **Brasillach:** Robert Brasillach (1909–45), French journalist and editor of the fascist newspaper *Je suis partout*. He was executed as a collaborator in 1945.

15 **Hitler Youth Quex:** a 1932 Nazi propaganda novel (*Hitlerjunge Quex*) based on the life of Herbert 'Quex' Norkus.

15 **André Bellessort (1866–1942):** French writer and poet.

16 **This, then, was our youth … regained:** a quote from Claude Jamet's memoir of Brasillach before the war.

16 **Julien Benda: (1867–1956):** French philosopher and novelist, author of *The Betrayal of the Intellectuals*.

16 **Maurras:** Charles Maurras (1868–1952), a French author and poet, was the principal thinker behind *Action Française*; a supporter of Vichy, he was arrested and sentenced to life imprisonment.

16 *Je suis partout:* (*I am everywhere*) a right wing anti-Semitic French newspaper founded by Jean Fayard in 1930. It supported the Nazis during the occupation and, during the war, was edited by Robert Brasillach.

16 **P.-A. Cousteau:** Pierre-Antoine Cousteau (1906–58), French far right journalist and contributor to *Je suis partout*.

17 **Pujo:** Maurice Pujo (1872–1955), French journalist and co-founder of the *Comité d'Action Française* which later became *Action Française*.

17 **Maxime Real del Sarte (1888–1954):** French sculptor and political activist involved with the right-wing *Action Française*.

17 **Jean Luchaire (1901–46):** French journalist and politician, later head of the French collaborationist press during the Nazi occupation. He was executed for collaborationism in 1946.

17 **Carlingue:** the informal name for the French Gestapo, which was headquartered on the Rue Lauriston.

17 **Brinon:** Fernand de Brinon (1884–1947), French lawyer and journalist, was among the principal architects of French collaboration with the Nazis. He was found guilty of war crimes in 1947 and executed.

17 **Abetz:** Otto Abetz (1903–58), the German ambassador to Vichy France during the Second World War.

17 **General Commissariat for Jewish Affairs:** *Commissariat général aux questions juives*, the administrative committee tasked with enforcing the anti-Semitic policies of the Vichy Government.

18 **Stülpnagel:** Otto von Stülpnagel (1878–1948), head of the occupied forces and military governor of Paris. He committed suicide while awaiting trial after the war.

18 **Doriot:** Jacques Doriot (1898–1945), Communist turned fascist who, with Marcel Déat, founded the *Légion des Volontaires Français*.

18 **Déat:** Marcel Déat (1894–1955), founder of the *Rassemblement national populaire* (National Popular Rally), a political party in the Vichy Government; later appointed Minister of Labour and National Solidarity.

18 **Jo Darnand:** Joseph Darnand (1897–1945), a decorated French soldier during the First World War, Darnand went on to become a leading collaborator during the Second World War, founding the collaborationist militia *Service d'ordre legionnaire*, which later became the *Milice*.

18 **Franc-Garde:** armed wing of the *Milice*. In 1943–44, it fought alongside the German army against the *Maquis*.

20 **… beautiful lines by Spire:** André Spire (1868–1966), French poet, and writer.

26 **L'Aiglon:** Napoleon II 'the Eaglet' who died aged twenty-one.

26 **Süss the Jew:** the eponymous character in the 1940 Nazi propaganda film *Jud Süß* commissioned by Joseph Goebbels.

27 **The 'Horst-Wessel-Lied':** song penned by Horst Wessel in 1929, usually known as 'Die Fahne hoch' ('The Flag on High'), it was adopted as the Nazi Party anthem in 1930.

28 **Colonel de la Rocque:** François de La Rocque (1885–1946), leader of the French right-wing *Croix de Feu* during the 1930s and later the French nationalist *Parti Social Français*.

30 **Brocéliande:** in French literature, a mythical forest said to be the last resting place of Merlin the magician.

31 **Tante Léonie:** character in Proust's *In Search Of Lost Time* at whose house Marcel stays in Combray.

31 **Maurice Dekobra (1885–1973):** French writer of adventure novels.

31 **Stavinsky:** Alexandre Stavinsky (1888–1934), French 'financier' with considerable influence among government ministers and bankers. After his death in 1934, it was discovered that he had embezzled 200 million francs from the Crédit municipal de Bayonne, a scandal which rocked the French government.

31 **Novarro:** Ramón Novarro (1899–1968), Mexican actor, one of the great stars of the silent cinema.

31 **the anti-Jewish exhibition at the Palais Berlitz:** *Le Juif et la France*, a notorious anti-Semitic propaganda exhibition staged in Paris during the Nazi occupation.

32 *Bagatelles pour un massacre*: title of a collection of virulently anti-Semitic essays by Louis-Ferdinand Céline, translated as *Trifles for a Massacre*.

35 **Rue d'Ulm! Rue d'Ulm!:** the address of the prestigious École Normale Supérieure.

35 **Jallez and Jephanion:** the writer Jallez and the politician Jephanion are the inseparable friends in Jules Romain's novel *Les Hommes de bonne volonté* (*The Men of Good Will*).

37 **to join the LVF:** *Légion des volontaires français (contre le bolchévisme)*, the Legion of French Volunteers (Against Bolshevism), a collaborationist French militia founded on July 8, 1941.

38 **Rastignac:** a character in Balzac's *La Comédie humaine*, Eugène de Rastignac is portrayed as a naïve but fervent social climber – he went by the name 'Rastignac de la butte Montmartre'.

38 **... to quote Péguy:** Charles Péguy (1873–1914), French poet and essayist, he coined the phrase 'les hussards noirs' in 1913 to refer to his teachers.

39 **He insisted that ... to notice him:** parodying the phrase 'if the Jew did not exist, the anti-Semite would invent him' in Sartre's *Anti-Semite and Jew*.

44 **my old friend Seingalt:** Casanova, who signed his *Memoirs* (as he did many other works) Jacques Casanova de Seingalt.

46 **Paul Chack (1876–1945):** French Naval officer and collaborationist writer.

46 **Monsignor Mayol de Lupé (1873–1955):** Catholic priest who served as chaplain for the *Légion des volontaires français* and later for the SS.

46 **Henri Béraud (1885–1958):** French novelist and journalist. Virulently Anglophobic and anti-Semitic, he supported the Vichy Government. After the liberation, he was sentenced to death for collaboration. The sentence was later commuted to life imprisonment.

46 **... attack on Mers-el-Kébir:** as a direct response to the signing of the French–German armistice, the British Navy bombarded the French Navy off the coast of Algeria in July 1940, resulting in the deaths of 1,297 French servicemen.

46 **'Maréchal, nous voilà':** a French song pledging loyalty to Maréchal Pétain.

48 *Romanciers du terroir*: a group of turn-of-the-century French novelists best known for their realistic depiction of rural life.

48 **Mistral:** Frédéric Mistral (1830–1914), French novelist awarded the Nobel Prize for Literature in 1904.

49 **Bichelonne:** Jean Bichelonne (1904–44), French businessman and civil servant, later head of the *Office central de repartition des produits industriels* in the Vichy government.

49 **Hérold-Paquis:** Jean Auguste Hérold aka Jean Hérold-Paquis (1912–45), a French journalist who fought for Franco during the Spanish Civil War and was later appointed Delegate for Propaganda to the Hautes-Alpes region by the Vichy Government. Executed for treason in 1945.

49 **admirals Esteva, Darlan and Platón:** three admirals who served in the Vichy regime.

50 **Joseph de Maistre (1753–1821):** Joseph-Marie, Comte de Maistre, philosopher and writer who famously defended the monarchy after the French Revolution.

56 **Maurice Barrès (1861–1923):** French symbolist writer, politician who popularised the notion of ethnic nationalism in France. An influential anti-Semite, he broke with the left wing to become a leading anti-Dreyfusard, writing: 'That Dreyfus is guilty, I deduce not from the facts themselves, but from his race.'

57 **Charles Martel (68?–741):** Frankish military leader who defeated Abdul Rahman's son, halting the advance of the Islamic caliphate circa 736.

57 **fleurs-de-lis on a field Azure:** the heraldic arms of 'France Ancienne'.

58 **I was secretary to Joanovici:** Joseph Joanovici (1905–65), a French Jewish iron supplier, who supplied both Nazi Germany and the French Resistance. After the war, he was found guilty of collaboration and sentenced to prison. In 1958 he escaped from France to Israel but was refused the right to request to naturalise and returned to France. He was released in 1962.

60 **Frison-Roche:** Roger Frison-Roche (1906–99), French mountaineer, explorer and novelist.

62 **Henry Bordeaux (1870–1963):** French lawyer, essayist and writer. His novels reflect the values of traditional provincial Catholic communities.

62 **Capitaine Danrit:** pen name of Émile Driant, (1855–1916), French writer, politician, and a decorated army officer. He died at the Battle of Verdun during the First World War.

66 **Édouard Drumont (1844–1917):** French journalist and writer who founded the Antisemitic League of France in 1889. He later founded and edited the French anti-Semitic political newspaper *La Libre Parole*.

67 **Each man in his darkness goes towards his Light:** a quotation from *Les Contemplations* by Victor Hugo.

71 **a new 'Curé d'Ars':** a reference to Saint John Vianney, a French parish priest, known as the Curé d'Ars.

72 *My heart, smile towards the future now* ...: from the poem 'La dure épreuve va finir' by Paul Verlaine.

72 *The fireside, the lamplight's slender beam:* from the poem 'Le foyer, la lueur étroite de la lampe' by Paul Verlaine.

72 *furia francese:* the 'French fury' – attributed to the French by the Italians at the Battle of Fornovo.

75 **Giraudoux's girls love to travel:** Jean Giraudoux (1882–1944), French novelist, essayist, diplomat and playwright.

75 **Charles d'Orléans (1691–1744):** eighteenth-century French man of letters.

75 **Maurice Scève (c. 1501–64):** French Renaissance poet much obsessed with spiritual love.

75 **Rémy Belleau (1528–77):** sixteenth-century French poet known for his paradoxical poems of praise for simple things.

79 **even a thousand Jews ... Body of Our Lord:** an oblique reference to the line in Proust's *Sodom and Gomorrah*: 'A strange Jew who boiled the Host'.

80 **They strolled together ... spring waters:** alluding to *Swann's Way*, the first volume of Proust's *In Search of Lost Time* where the narrator dreams that Mme de Guermantes will show him the grounds of her house.

80 **'The energy and charm ... eyes of rabbits':** paraphrasing a passage from Proust's *The Guermantes Way*.

81 *The Embarkation of Eleanor of Aquitaine for the Orient:* an allusion to Claude Lorrain's 1648 painting *The Embarkation of the Queen of Sheba*.

81 *The Fougeire-Jusquiames Way*: alluding to *Swann's Way* by Marcel Proust. The passage that Modiano follows offers a variation on the Proustian bedtime scenes of Combray.

82 **the Princesse des Ursins:** Marie Anne de La Trémoille, a lady at the Spanish Court during the reign of Philip V.

82 **Mlle de la Vallière:** Louise de La Vallière (1644–1710), mistress of Louis XIV.

82 **Mme Soubise:** Anne de Rohan-Chabot, a mistress of Louis XIV.

82 *La Belle aux cheveux d'or*: a story by Countess d'Aulnoy usually translated as *The Story of Pretty Goldilocks* or *The Beauty with Golden Hair*.

82 **'It was, this "Fougeire-Jusquiames," ... with heraldic details':** paraphrasing *The Guermantes Way* by Marcel Proust.

84 **Arno Breker (1900–91):** German sculptor, whose public works in Nazi Germany were praised as expressions of the 'mighty momentum and will power' ('Wucht und Willenhaftigkeit').

86 **The still pale moonlight, sad and fair:** from the poem 'Clair de Lune' by Paul Verlaine.

88 **Perhaps too, in these last days ... anti-Semitic propaganda had revived:** a quote from *Sodom and Gomorrah* by Marcel Proust.

89 **The Jew is the substance of God ... only a mare:** a parody of the nineteenth-century anti-Semitic text *Der Talmud Jüde*, by August Rohling, a professor at the German University of Prague.

92 **'Hitlerleute':** 'Hitler's people' – a fascist song using the same tunes as the official hymn of the Italian National Fascist Party.

93 **Baldur von Schirach (1907–74):** Nazi youth leader later convicted of crimes against humanity.

95 **Marizibill:** title of a poem by Guillaume Apollinaire about a prostitute in Cologne and her Jewish pimp.

96 **Zarah Leander (1907–81):** Swedish singer and actress whose greatest success was in Germany during the 1930s and 1940s.

97 **Skorzeny:** Otto Skorzeny (1908–75), served as SS-Standartenführer in the German Waffen-SS during the Second World War.

102　**the phosphorus of Hamburg:** the allied bombs dropped on Hamburg during the Second World War contained phosphorus.

103　**'Einheitsfrontlied':** 'The United Front Song', (by Bertolt Brecht and Hanns Eisler), one of the best-known songs of the German workers' movement.

103　**the anthem of the Thälmann-Kolonne:** the anti-fascist song, 'Die Thälmann-Kolonne', also known as 'Spaniens Himmel' ('Spanish skies'), was a communist anthem.

104　**Julius Streicher (1885–1946):** a prominent Nazi, the founder and publisher of the newspaper *Der Stürmer*. In 1946 he was convicted of crimes against humanity and executed.

105　**the traitorous Prince Laval:** Pierre Laval (1883–1945), prime minister of France during the Third Republic, later a member of the Vichy government. After the liberation he was convicted of high treason and executed.

107　**'I will not be home tonight ... black and white':** alluding to the suicide note left by Gérard de Nerval for his aunt. 'Ne m'attends pas ce soir car la nuit sera noire et blanche.'

110　**Say, what have you done ... with your youth?:** the last line of the poem 'Le Ciel est, par-dessus le toit' by Paul Verlaine.

113　**the roundup on 16 July 1942:** The Vel' d'Hiv Roundup was a Nazi-ordered mass arrest of Parisian Jews by the French police.

116　**Émilienne d'Alençon (1869–1946):** French dancer and actress. She was famously a courtesan, and the lover of, among others, Leopold II of Belgium.

119　**'When I hear the word culture, I reach for my truncheon':** alluding to the line 'when I hear the word culture, I reach for my gun' often attributed to Hermann Göring. In fact, the line originally appears in Hanns Johst's play *Schlageter*: 'Whenever I hear the word Culture ... I release the safety catch of my Browning!'

129　**'Du bist der Lenz nachdem ich verlangte':** 'You are the spring for which I longed' – Sieglinde's aria from Richard Wagner's opera *Die Walküre*.

130 **Radio Londres:** a BBC broadcast in French to occupied France during the Second World War.

138 *Moi, j'aime le music-hall … danseuses légères*: 'Moi j'aime le music hall' by Charles Trenet.

THE NIGHT WATCH

WINNER OF THE NOBEL PRIZE FOR LITERATURE

When Patrick Modiano was awarded the 2014 Nobel Prize for Literature he was praised for using the 'art of memory' to bring to life the Occupation of Paris during the Second World War.

The Night Watch is the story of a young man of limited means caught between his work for the French Gestapo informing on the Resistance and his work for a Resistance cell informing on the police and the black market dealers whose seedy milieu of nightclubs, prostitutes and spivs he shares. Under pressure from both sides to betray the other, he finds himself forced to devise an escape route out of an impossible situation – how to be a traitor without being a traitor.

'Modiano is the poet of the Occupation and a spokesman for the disappeared, and I am thrilled that the Swedish Academy has recognised him'
Rupert Thomson

ORDER BY PHONE: +44 (0)1256 302 699; BY EMAIL: DIRECT@MACMILLAN.CO.UK

DELIVERY IS USUALLY 3–5 WORKING DAYS. FREE POSTAGE AND PACKAGING FOR ORDERS OVER £20.

ONLINE: WWW.BLOOMSBURY.COM/BOOKSHOP

PRICES AND AVAILABILITY SUBJECT TO CHANGE WITHOUT NOTICE.

WWW.BLOOMSBURY.COM/PATRICKMODIANO

BLOOMSBURY

RING ROADS

WINNER OF THE NOBEL PRIZE FOR LITERATURE

Ring Roads is a brilliant, almost hallucinatory evocation of the uneasy, corrupt years of the French Occupation. It tells the story of a young Jewish man in search of the father who disappeared from his life ten years earlier. Serge finds Chalva trying to survive the war years in the unlikely company of black marketeers, anti-Semites and prostitutes, putting his meagre and not entirely orthodox business skills at the service of those who have little interest in his survival.

Savage in its depiction of the anti-Semitic newspaper editor, the bullying ex-Foreign Legionnaire who treats Chalva with ever more threatening contempt,
what makes *Ring Roads* exceptional is Modiano's empathy for a man who cannot see the danger he courts.

'Subtle, rhythmic, and hypnotic investigations into the self and its memory'
SLATE.COM

ORDER BY PHONE: +44 (0)1256 302 699; BY EMAIL: DIRECT@MACMILLAN.CO.UK

DELIVERY IS USUALLY 3–5 WORKING DAYS. FREE POSTAGE AND PACKAGING FOR ORDERS OVER £20.

ONLINE: WWW.BLOOMSBURY.COM/BOOKSHOP

PRICES AND AVAILABILITY SUBJECT TO CHANGE WITHOUT NOTICE.

WWW.BLOOMSBURY.COM/PATRICKMODIANO

B L O O M S B U R Y